FIRST ROUND

Linc looked across the diner and saw a monstrous human hulk coming toward him. The giant was easily six foot seven and had to weigh three hundred pounds at least — most of it in his massive chest, shoulders, and arms. He stood at the table, looming over Linc and his son like a giant redwood. 'You Silver Hawk?'

Very amicably, Linc said, 'Yeah.'

'I'm the Smasher. Looka here, Silver Hawk, how'd you like to wrestle me?'

Linc looked him up and down and scratched his shoulders and neck and considered it. 'I don't know. Maybe we oughta wait till we meet in Vegas, huh?'

'What's a matter? I got too much weight for you? Outta your class?'

'Hey, man, I been drivin' for hours. I just ordered my steaks. My boy here is hungry. Gimme a break, huh?'

Smasher growled, 'All I been hearing lately on the road is Silver Hawk, Silver Hawk, Silver Hawk — he's the dude to beat.' He threw two fingers down on the table, pressing firmly, 'Two out of three, okay?' he asked, pushing for the match.

Linc rubbed his stomach and looked across the room, ignoring the Smasher. 'Make it just one. One's okay.'

Joel Humphreys

Futura

ISBN 0 7088 3381 0

Set in IBM Journal by ℱ Tek Art Ltd
Croydon, Surrey

Printed in Great Britain by
Hazell, Watson and Viney Ltd
Aylesbury, Bucks

Futura Publications
A Division of
Macdonald & Co (Publishers) Ltd
Greater London House
Hampstead Road
London NW1 7QX

A BPCC plc Company

CHAPTER ONE

Somewhere near the Virginia border it started snowing. Big, lazy Appalachian Mountain flakes fluttered down on the highway.

The windshield wipers of the tractor-trailer rig slapped at the splattering flakes. But the driver paid no mind.

The barrier railings flickered by as he took the winding curves with little effort, seemingly unconcerned with the two-hundred-foot plunge beyond. At the bottom lay the misty bed of the Jackson River.

Despite the danger, the driver rode the outer flank of the road. As he brought the rig out on a brief straighaway, the majestic profile of the machine revealed itself against the natural beauty of the mountains.

On the driver's door a giant silver hawk flew, its wings outspread. Below the bird was the name of the driver-owner and -operator: Lincoln Hawks.

At thirty-two, Hawks' skin was smooth as the polished metal of his Volvo-White truck. He was ruggedly handsome with high cheekbones prominent over a short beard. His black hair was straight. He looking slightly Indian, especially in profile.

His eyes were black, intense, and alert. Even in a plaid winter jacket, blue jeans, and trucker boots, his sculptured body was evident to the most causual observer. His head-gear was unusual. Instead of the standard 'gimme' cap,

1

Hawks' had a bright red headband with hand-embroidered Indian symbols.

He was not a giant man, even though the rolled-up sleeves of his jacket revealed powerful, muscular forearms and wrists. Looking at him sitting in the truck, one would expect him to be much bigger — probably because of his thick neck and chest.

Untroubled by the hazardous wintry weather beating against the windshield, he drove with his left arm only.

He kept the other arm busy with exercises. As Johnny Cash throbbed from the dual speakers in the cab, Hawks pulled a brace of steel-reinforced, maxi-strength rubber cords toward his chest from a special mounting on the dashboard.

The strong rubber resisted the pull, but the powerful arm continued relentlessly toward Hawks' chest. The rubber stretched. The bicep bulged. He held the tension on the straining rubber bands, holding the handle to his chest.

His dark eyes were riveted to the highway. The snow continued to fall as Johnny Cash sang. The big rig rumbled onward, consuming the road. And Lincoln Hawks' arm continued to hold. When he decided he had held long enough, the arm unlatched, slowly releasing the pull. Once completing the exercise, he repeated it again and again. He judged the length of an exercise by the music playing. When one side of the cassette had finished, he stopped, flipped it over, and started a new set.

Having listened to both sides of Cash's *Bitter Tears* album — ballads of the American Indian — he ended the exercises and slipped a Kenny Rogers tape into the machine.

He relaxed his arm to Rogers' singing about the dangers of falling in love with a dreamer. The right arm was swelling with blood and feeling tight. He shook it, wiggled his fingers, and stretched the pumped muscles with which he intended to fulfill his dreams.

As he rotated his neck to relieve tension, he caught a flash of white in the port-side mirror. He took the steering wheel in both hands and studied the source of the light. A long-haul truck was bearing down from behind.

Linc kicked more fuel to the engine and eyed the truck rushing down upon him at incredible speed.

'What the shit's he doing?' he mumbled to himself.

His eyes cut back to the mirrors. He pushed the truck a little faster, wondering to himself, *Does that idiot intend to pass or what? But what else can he be intending? Run up my ass?*

Then it occurred to him that maybe the poor bastard was in trouble. Maybe the driver's passed out, he thought.

A puzzled frown creased his forehead. He didn't like it. No fool would be coming at that speed deliberately. Something was wrong. 'Shit,' he growled as the huge steel bumpers raced toward him, filling his mirror.

Linc's eyes jumped back to the road. His options were few. He had to make a decision, and he didn't have much time. He had to make it fast. The bastard was almost on him. The wipers flip-flopped back and forth, scraping snow from the windshield. Linc could see the road ahead veering sharply to the left, winding around the mountain. Beyond the curve there was nothing but space and the deep drop into the valley.

Linc was highballing it already, but he pushed it faster. Kenny Rogers sang on.

Linc bucked in his seat. He couldn't believe it. The crazy son of a bitch had rammed him. He felt another jolt and a sudden surge of power that took him toward the edge of the mountain.

The bumper slammed against his trailer again, knocking him almost out of his seat.

'Damn,' he gasped as he floorboarded the accelerator.

3

The big engine responded, and Linc started to pull away. Linc's White hit the curve at full speed. He gripped the steering wheel with a soft touch, leaning in his seat like a race-car driver on a hot turn and brought the big baby out of the curve several yards ahead of the pursuing truck.

But as Linc came out of the straightaway, he saw in his mirror that the maniac was still bearing down, trying to close the gap. Linc's big engine was powerful. On the straightaway he pulled away, but only far enough to keep from being slammed from behind.

At the next curve the maniac's intent became clear. It was no runaway. No accident. The bastard was trying to force Linc off the road, trying to cause an accident.

Linc realized the other driver meant to kill him — as surely as if he were pointing a loaded gun.

As they hit the turn, the other truck bore down again, trying to move up on the outside and take the middle of the highway, forcing Linc toward the railing. It was a game of king of the mountain. The loser would take a rocky ride down the canyon wall.

Instinctively, Linc's reflexes snapped into action. Without a thought, except of survival, he whipped the wheel to the left, pulling the big load into the center of the two-lane highway. He had to get off the edge. He couldn't ride the rail, where the slightest bump would send him hurtling into space. In the middle of the highway he could deny the attacker room to maneuver. There would be no way he could control him there.

But at that moment Linc's eyes picked up the sight of an oncoming car in the distance.

Linc screamed in disbelief, 'Son of a bitch!' Behind him a maniac was trying to force him off the road. If he gave the middle of the highway to the oncoming car, he was a dead man. If he stayed in the middle, the innocent motorist didn't have a chance.

4

As if the driver could hear him, Linc started to yell at the approaching car, 'Get outta the way! Get outta the way!'

He hit the horn for all it was worth. The horn blasted out, blaring nonstop. As the two vihicles grew nearer, Linc realized the other driver wans't responding. Maybe he was frozen in fear. Linc zigged the big rig back into his lane and let the oncoming car have the road.

From behind, the maniac trucker gunned his motor, taking advantage of the move to pull up and push Linc off the mountain. But he couldn't avoid the station wagon.

Linc heard the squealing tires and then the crash, followed by a thunderous explosion that rocked his rig. He could hear the station wagon scraping along the wall of the mountain.

The maniac's truck was a runaway. It jackknifed and ricocheted across the highway, screeching like a wounded animal. Skidding across the asphalt, it slammed against the railing and snapped it like a matchstick, then flew off the mountain and into space.

Linc slowly eased his own rig to a roll. Being careful not to brake too quickly on the wet road, he came to a stop well away from the accident and flipped on the caution blinkers.

He ran toward the sickening scene. Scattered about the highway were remnants of the crash — a hubcap, smashed glass, bits of metal, a man's hat, and a pair of glasses.

Pinned against the mountain was the blazing wreckage of the station wagon. Linc stopped running. Stunned by the sight, he hesitated, rubbed his eyes to clear them from the heat and smoke. Inside the burning car he could see the remains of what moments before had been a human being.

Linc moved closer for a better look, shielding his face and eyes with his forearm. There was nothing he could do.

There was no one to help.

He turned and moved across the road to the edge of the highway, stopping to look down in the deep, misty canyon where the unknown maniac driver had so fervently tried to send him. At the bottom he saw the smoking remains of the truck.

Linc exhaled and shook his head. He blinked his eyes, then turned and jogged back to the Silver Hawk.

He grabbed the CB mike and stretched the cord out the door. He needed fresh air. He wanted its coolness on his face. He needed the truck to lean against.

'Breaker . . . breaker . . . this is Silver Hawk calling Smoky. I'm reporting a ten-fifty major.'

Over the radio he heard an official-sounding voice respond, 'This is the Virginia State Police, Silver Hawk. Trooper Johnson speaking. What's your twenty, Silver Hawk?'

'I'm at the four-fifteen yardstick,' Linc said with a gush of energy in his voice, 'on State 306 — headed north.'

'We copy, Silver Hawk. Are there injuries?'

'Negatory,' said Linc. 'Not this time. For this one you can send a one-way camper.' His voice trailed off at the end of the message.

'We do not copy, Silver Hawk. Say again,' responded the trooper.

Linc hesitated, still leaning against the cab of the truck. He bent forward, thinking about the reply.

He finally pushed himself upright and brought the microphone to his mouth again. He sighed and answered softly this time, 'A four-wheeler and an eighteen-wheeler got together — head on. Nobody walked away.'

'Please stand by, Silver Hawk. We're on the way.'

Linc waited. He leaned back his head and looked up at the snow cascading down on him, the flakes splashing to wetness against his face. He spoke into the mike once more.

6

'Yeah, ten-four,' he said.

He stared down the highway at the burning wreckage and gripped the mike tightly, rubbing his knuckles against his forehead. He straightened his back, folded his arms in front of his chest and stood defiantly rigid, still staring at the burning car.

His heart was pounding like a hammer. Fury was building inside him. He was controlling it, keeping it just below the surface — but not too far below the surface.

CHAPTER TWO

Michael Cutler was a strange boy, thin and bookish and humorless. At age twelve he had become something between a robot and a good little soldier. Blessed with superior intelligence and a gift for the technical, he could have easily been classified a nerd, but the nerds wouldn't have claimed, him, even if he'd been thrown in with them.

He was a loner, a boy used to having his own way. He had never been denied anything, not even at the Virginia Military Institute. He'd always had everything he wanted — his way. He was spoiled rotten, obnoxious, and generally a first-class pain in the ass. But he didn't know it. He never even thought about it. He was used to things being the way he wanted them. That was just the way things were when you were the grandson of one of the richest men in the world. His grandfather, Jason Cutler, the Texas oil and real-estate tycoon, always saw to it that Michael received what he wanted, even at VMI. No one bucked Jason Cutler. He was too rich and too powerful. In turn, no one crossed little Michael Cutler because of the grandfather's awesome power.

At VMI Michael had his way. He had his own room while the other cadets shared. He had his own individual shower stall. The other boys shared showers. His room was filled with all the modern conveniences and specialities befitting a young genius. He had his own specially designed module wall unit for his computer system. Even his bath soap was imported from Paris.

As unbelievable as it was, the strange, pathetic boy was the flesh-and-blood son of Lincoln Hawk.

This plastic-programmed little stiff-neck monster was part of Lincoln Hawk's dream. He was the reason for Linc's speeding through Virginia. He was on his way to claim his son, even if it meant colliding with the awesome power of Jason Cutler.

Unaware of the changes about to occur in his life, Michael stood in the parade grounds at attention. Like his classmates, he was decked out in full-dress uniform for the morning parade.

Friday afternoon meant parade, even for Michael Cutler. But Michael never tried in any way to dismiss or sidestep his responsibilities as a good cadet.

He was a good student and model member of the elite corps at VMI.

The only thing that differentiated Michael Cutler from his classmates on parade day was that when the call to dismiss rang across the grounds, all the other cadets screamed and charged across the grounds, yanking at their ties, eager to change clothes and hit the road for home.

Michael was above all that. Screaming and running, grinning and laughing were too childish for him. He walked to his room with the dignity and class of a good cadet. He never had any parents at the parade grounds to run to anyway. Grandfather Cutler sent the limo to pick him up and rush him to the airport. How else would he get home to Texas for the weekend?

In the showers the boys joked and talked about their plans for the weekend — the ball games, the movies, the parties, the games they would play. The room vibrated with the boys' anticipation of a fun weekend.

Then Michael Cutler entered the room. It was like a cloud

passing over the sun. It was like a cop visiting a Hell's Angels picnic. A wet blanket had come to the party.

The other cadets paused in their conversations and watched him walk past. The temperature of the room dropped ten degrees, but the handsome dark-haired boy in the silk robe from Belgium never felt the chill. He was oblivious to it. He was in his own world. He wouldn't have understood, even if he'd noticed. He was minding his business. They were expected to mind theirs. He had little time for foolishness or juvenile pranks. To him, his peers were simply immature children.

He walked past the boys who were waiting for the showers. The fact that four boys were waiting in line ahead of him didn't mean he had to wait. It was understood. He would have his shower. Then, and only then, would the other boys have theirs.

He stepped into the shower and shut the door. From inside the shower he draped his robe on the hook outside and spread the towel across the top of the shower door. Then he turned on the water, and steam started to rise inside the stall. It was then that the boys' true feelings started to show.

Randy Charles, a mischievous kid almost as wide as he was tall with a gift for pantomime, started his imitation of young Mr. Cutler.

As he pranced and posed and raised his nose high in the air, his classmates snickered and grinned and tried to keep from guffawing right out loud. All of the boys, of course, wanted to give the little brat a kick in the ass, a punch in the nose, at least a good old 'up yours, Pal,' but they didn't dare. They were good soldiers doing as they were told. They had learned the hard way that it was a no-win situation dealing with Michael Cutler. Even if you won, you lost. The price was too high. They simply accepted the unpleasant situation. It was like bad weather. You didn't

11

like it, but you made the most of it. It was useless to gripe or complain. Just accept it and learn to live with it.

Toby Carlson, a freckle-faced redhead from Oklahoma and the son of a Methodist preacher, turned to his buddy, Dax Monroe, the senator's kid from West Virginia, and said, 'Hey, you ever think maybe he ain't a he? Maybe he's a she.'

Dax grinned and held a finger in front of his lips to indicate that he'd better be quiet and not let Michael hear him.

Toby stuck out his tongue to show his disregard and sneered, 'I bet the reason he never showers with us is because he ain't got a dick. That's why he wants to cover up all the time.'

Dax shook with laughter, as did several other boys who had heard the remark. At least they laughed until the door to the shower opened. Then their faces fell blank.

Michael stepped from the shower with the silk robe belted tightly at his waist. The imported soap bar from Paris hung from his neck. He marched past his fellow cadets with nary a nod.

Once out the door, the room exploded with laughter. Randy Charles was shaking his butt and sashaying in front of the shower in imitation of Michael. He opened the shower door with two fingers and entered, holding his nose high.

Outside in the school parking lot, Lincoln Hawks guided his fifty-footer through the parents' traffic of BMW and Mercedes sedans, all bearing their loads of children away for the weekend.

After finally clearing enough space to park the big, burdensome rig, Linc eased the baby to a stop and killed the engine and set the brakes.

He jumped to the ground with a brown manila envelope in his hand and slapped it against his thigh. The air was brisk

12

and the sky was clear. He had left the snow behind in the mountains.

He studied the buildings, trying to decide which direction to move. As he took his first step, a young cadet, carrying an overnight bag and clarinet case, collided with the trucker. The boy bounced off Linc and hit the ground flat on his butt.

'Sorry, sir,' said the stunned kid from his resting place on the ground.

Linc bent down and pulled the boy to his feet. 'Sorry nothing,' said Linc. 'The foul was on me. You had the right to the lane.' The boy grinned and rose to his feet. 'Thank you, sir,' he said and hurried on toward a car.

Linc watched him go.

He liked what he saw. The kid made him feel good. He sighed and wondered if the meeting with his own son would have any warmth at all. Any smiles? Any jokes? He didn't know. But he was going to find out.

As he turned to go, he heard a young voice ask, 'Is that yours?'

Linc turned and saw the source of the question, a tiny half-pint kid pointing at the rig.

Linc grinned. 'Yeah, I guess you could call it mine. I only got six more payments to go on it.'

A skinny, tough-looking friend with a chipped tooth said, 'You really sleep in that thing?'

'Not when I'm driving,' said Linc.

The skinny tough gave him a sneer to let Linc know he wasn't funny. They might be VMI military boys, but they were still boys. They didn't have to listen to some jerk's lame jokes.

'Sorry,' said Linc. 'Just a . . . never mind. Stay cool,' he said and started walking.

'Hey,' yelled the little one. 'Can we see inside?'

'I'd like to show it to you guys, but I'm running late

13

already. Missed the parade and everything. Got held up on the road. Really, I need to go. Later maybe.'

'Sure,' shrugged the skinny friend. 'C'mon,' he said to his little buddy. They turned and walked away.

Linc tilted his head and shrugged. What the hell, he thought. You can't please everybody.

Michael was in his room. He stood at the bed and fumbled with the articles he was packing for the weekend. He checked his bag one last time to make sure he had everything. It seemed to be all there. He glanced around the room. Unlike the other boys at VMI, who shared rooms, Michael was sole proprietor and master of his universe. The room held only one bunk. On the other side of the room, where it was customary for the roommate's bunk to be, a special work module had been built, and along the intersecting wall, ceiling-to-floor built-in bookshelves had been constructed.

In the work module was an IBM microcomputer, complete with printer. Included in the wall as part of the unit was a set of neatly labeled steel files.

On the nightstand beside Michael's bed were the only strictly personal touches in the room. A picutre of his mother had been placed facing his bed. Beside her picture was a second photograph. It was of himself as a very young boy decked out in a cowboy costume — big black hat, boots, chaps, vest, jeans, and an embroidered shirt. The picture was reminiscent of the photos that grace the homes of young cowboys and cowgirls all over America — the Shetland pony pose.

Only, Michael's western picture was posed not on the back of a Shetland pony, but astride a beautiful Arabian stallion. In addition, Michael was holding the silver pommel of a hand-tooled western saddle. Standing beside him in the picture was the man responsible for the horse and the

14

saddle and all the luxuries in the boy's room — the million-aire grandfather, Jason Cutler, a rugged, proud man with silver hair and gray, cold eyes of steel.

Except for the two pictures, Michael's room might just have easily have been an isolated corner at the main library. It was not a room to live in. Not a place to relax or enjoy. It was an office, a work space. It was the spartan room of a bookworm.

The young bookworm was zipping his travel bag when he heard a knock at the door.

'Yes?' he said.

The door opened gently, and a young cadet in T-shirt and shorts stuck his head into the room.

'What is it, Barney?' asked Michael.

'I was just wondering if it would be all right for me to use your computer while you're out of town. I'm staying here this weekend. I have a program that I need to —'

'No,' said Michael, not bothering to listen to the rest of the explanation.

'But my semester project —'

Again Michael did not dignify the young man's explanation. He raised his head and looked at the boy for the first time during the conversation. He lifted his bag from the bed and moved toward the door. In a soft voice with no emotion, Michael answered him again.

'I told you, Barney. The answer is no. Please get out of the door. I have to lock up and leave.'

'What's the matter?' protested Barney, backing out of the room. 'You think I'll break it or something?'

Michael followed him out the door and locked it behind him.

'No one is allowed near my data files or my spread sheets. You might wipe out programs I'm working on.'

'I'm not an idiot, ya know.'

Michael turned and walked away. He did not bother to

15

say good-bye.

As Barney watched him exit down the corridor, he said his good-bye to young Mr. Cutler — with his middle finger.

'I understand fully,' said Colonel Davis. Davis was on the telephone, double-checking what he had just heard. Davis, a balding man in his fifties, was a dedicated teacher. He knew he had to be particularly careful with anything concerning the Cutler boy. His grandfather was one of the country's richest and most powerful men and he'd been hinting lately about donating an impressive amount of money to the school.

Jonathan Davis could have retired to a ranch and written his memoirs, or he could have taken one of the many job opportunities offered him after his retirement. Instead he chose to stay with the military life and be close to young men — the future soldiers and leaders of the country he loved.

'No, ma'am, that is exactly what he told me,' he said, glancing across his desk at Lincoln Hawks. 'I just wanted to double-check it with you. I shall handle it exactly that way. No, everything will be fine. You have my assurance. Now you get some rest. And I'm sorry for disturbing you. My very best wishes and prayers will be with you next week. I know everything will turn out fine. Thank you. Good-bye now.'

Colonel Davis dropped the phone into its cradle and opened a palm toward Linc.

'She confirmed everything. Just as you said. I'll get the boy for you.'

He flipped the switch on the intercom. 'Have the officer of the day bring Cadet Michael Cutler to my office. Right away. He's scheduled to leave for the airport.'

16

Outside Michael's dormitory, a long black limo was idling. Michael strolled down the sidewalk toward the waiting car, gently swinging the small bag in his right hand. As he neared the car, a small black man with a salt-and-pepper pencil-thin mustache hopped from the car and hurried toward the boy.

When the two met on the sidewalk, the uniformed driver reached out for the boy's bag.

'Good afternoon sir,' said the driver.

'Hello,' said Michael, letting the bag slip from his hand to the driver's.

The driver hurried ahead of the boy and opened the back door of the limo. Michael strolled toward the door being held open for him. For Michael, services being performed for him by adults were something he accepted — even expected. He paid no more attention to it than most boys his age paid to receiving change at the supermarket.

As Michael ducked his head to climb into the limo, he heard someone call his name.

'Cutler!'

He stopped, stood up, and turned to see an upperclassman coming his way. On the arm of the upperclassman was an arm band labeled OFFICER OF THE DAY. The OD quickened his steps. Realizing who the upperclassman was, Michael immediately responded like the good cadet he was and saluted the officer. Just as crisply the OD returned the salute.

'The colonel want to see you in his office. On the double.'

Michael almost forwned, but he checked his emotions and in proper military fashion responded to the upper-classman.

'Sir, I believe that the colonel is aware that I am to meet my grandfather's plane . . .' The boy paused and checked his watch, a Rolex, and continued, 'In less than thirty minutes.'

17

'That is something to discuss with the colonel,' said the officer of the day. 'My order was to bring you to his office. Now, let's go.'

Michael did not like it, but he had no options. He sighed and replied, 'Yes, sir,' to the boy and walked away toward the administration building.

The OD took the bag from the driver's hand.

'He may need this,' he said, following in step behind Michael Cutler. The driver shut the limo door and watched the two boys enter the administration building. As they moved inside, the driver returned to his seat in the idling limo and killed the engine.

CHAPTER THREE

Lincoln Hawks was trying to conceal his emotions. He wanted to be cool, but instead he fidgeted, eaten up with nerves. His stomach felt like two dogs were inside it fighting over a bone. On the one hand, he knew that everything he'd worked for and thought about for the past ten years was tied up in the meeting. However, he didn't want to convey that to the boy. He wanted to be a regular guy. But how could he be a regular guy? The boy had never even seen him. His son probably wouldn't even recognize him. How do you causally start up a conversation with a twelve-year-old son who wouldn't know you from Adam?

Those were the thoughts spinning in Linc's mind and causing his stomach to roll like the ocean's tide.

He couldn't sit and he couldn't stand, so he paced. Colonel Davis said nothing, but he was well aware of the conflict and anxiousness being experienced by the man in his office. He watched Linc's shifting, restless energy. Their eyes met, and Linc realized that he was making a spectacle of himself. An embarrassed, nervous grin curved at Linc's mouth. Davis smiled back at him.

'Little nervous, I guess,' said Linc.

'Understandably,' said Davis. 'I have two boys of my own. I can imagine what you're feeling.'

There was a knock at the door.

'Come in,' said the colonel.

The door opened and Michael Cutler entered the room.

19

Linc's eyes cut to the boy immediately. His son. This handsome, frail boy was his son.

Michael came immediately to attention. He stood ramrod straight. His manner was serious and proper. Linc was impressed.

'The colonel wishes to see me.'

Colonel Davis looked up from his desk at the boy. Nervously, his fingers turned a ball-point pen over and over as he spoke.

'Yes. Your father wishes to see you, cadet.'

Michael immediately grimaced at the suggestion. The reaction on his face was unmistakable. The idea was distasteful to him, to say the least.

'My father?' he asked dumbfoundedly.

'He's going to drive you to Texas.'

'Hello, Mike,' said Linc softly.

At the sound of the voice, Michael turned slowly — very slowly — to look at the man behind him. The man he had not even noticed. The sight of the strange creature behind him was hard to believe. Were they serious? he thought. This wild man? This was supposed to be his father? It had to be some mistake. But something inside the boy said it was no mistake. Something deep down inside, beyond the shock and revulsion, sensed that this was the man he had be told about. This was the weirdo his grandfather had warned him about. It was his father, he knew it. But at the same time there was still programmed into his very being the belief that a father did not exist for him He had no father. That's what he had been told, that's what he believed, and that's the way it was.

Linc looked at the boy with the same tender, confused, proud, raw emotions bubbling in his eyes and dancing in his heart that every father feels when he peeps through the maternity glass to see the tiny, wrinkled, red-skinned, flannel-wrapped bundle of joy called a baby boy.

If someone had wanted to illustrate the word 'Love,' a snapshot of Linc looking at Michael would have done the job. He wore the evidence of his feelings on his smiling face. In his heart he wanted to swoop down on the boy like a giant hawk, wrap his powerful arms around his son, and squeeze and hug him. He wanted to hold him so close that the past ten years would fade away. He wanted the father and the son to be one — together. The distance, the separation, the lies and heartache he wanted to squeeze into oblivion, never to be remembered again. But he knew that was not possible. He knew those were the fantasies of a lonely father. He knew that reality forbid him from even touching the boy. He told himself to stay cool. He did not want to do anything that might shatter his possible future relationship with the boy. He wanted the boy to love him. He wanted the boy to feel the love he felt.

But the words that came from Michael gave no indication of any hope for a loving future with the boy.

The boy stated flatly and firmly, 'I have no father.'

It was not that he spat the words out to hurt Linc. He was not being nasty and cruel. The kid intended nothing by the remark. It was simply the readout from his computer. It was a cold and clinical statement expressing his beliefs. The boy's emotionless manner made the remark all the more painful for Linc.

But despite the pain he was feeling, Linc refused to let his happy face fall or fade away. He had prepared for the moment for too long. It would take more than a few body punches to turn him back.

However, the remark did bring a quick retort from Colonel Davis.

'*This* is your father, Michael.'

Michael gave him nothing. He tilted his head towards the man in the headband and considered him for a moment. There was still no hint of expression on his face, no indication of emotion in his voice as he replied to the colonel, 'Not to me he's not.'

Then, as if to dismiss Linc from the conversation, to close him out of the room, and for that matter, to exorcise him from his life, he turned his back on Linc and stood facing the colonel.

'Sir,' he said, addressing the colonel, 'my grandfather has instructed me that under no circumstances am I ever to be taken from this school by anyone other than himself or my mother. I believe if you will check my file you will find those instructions are a part of my conditions for enrollment here.'

The colonel answered him sharply, 'Your mother has legal custody over you, Cutler, *not* your grandfather.'

But the boy was resourceful and determined. Never displaying anything but cool calculation, he flexed muscles that few twelve-year-olds can muster against an adult, much less the head of their school. He said, 'With all respect, sir, I'm going to have to verify that.'

Without a second of hesitation or the slightest indication of irritation, the colonel said, 'I would expect you to,' and immediately he started to dial the telephone.

Linc said nothing. There was nothing for him to do, except to stand by and watch the tennis ball zing back and forth between the colonel and the boy.

The colonel continued talking as he dialed, explaining to the boy, 'Your mother told me just moments ago you'd insist on speaking with her. She's standing by for your call.'

He brought the phone receiver to his ear and said, 'Yes, this is Colonel Davis again. I'm putting Michael on.' He extended the phone toward the boy.

For a moment the boy hesitated, then he stepped forward, took the phone, and turned his back to Linc, deliberately shielding his father from the conversation.

'Is it the truth, Mother?' he whispered into the phone.

He sighed and asked, 'Must I?'

Linc could not hear the mother's words. Nor could he see the boy's face. He could not see the tears welling in the boy's eyes and spilling onto his cheeks. He could barely hear the boy's anguished question to the mother, 'But why?'

Linc looked at the floor and rubbed the carpet with the toe of his boot. The colonel looked down at his desk.

Michael squeezed his eyes shut and listened to his mother's pleading words to do as she had instructed, if for no other reason than that she was asking him. 'Please do it for me,' she pleaded. 'Just do it for me, Michael.' She paused and added, 'I love you.'

Michael swallowed and wiped his hand over the tears on his face and said, 'I love you too, Mama.'

He handed the phone back to the colonel. He diverted his eyes, refusing to look at him. Then the boy took a deep breath and turned to face the stranger he was supposed to recognize as his father.

'May I see some identification, sir?' asked Michael.

Aghast at the rude, insensitive behavior of the boy, Colonel Davis barked out, 'Cutler!'

But before the colonel could finish his reprimand, Linc stepped forward, waving his hand.

'It's all right, sir. It's all right. I came prepared.' From the brown manila envelope, he slipped an eight-by-ten photograph and handed it to Michael.

The boy took the photo and studied it. It was clearly a picture of his mother on her wedding day — and the man beside her was the man standing in the room with him.

He handed the picture back to Linc, but still he did not accept the situation without one final try at getting himself off the hook.

'Why are we driving? Why don't we just fly?' asked the boy.

'I just delivered a shipment to Richmond, so I was in the neighborhood. Your mother figured it would be a chance for us to get to know each other.'

'It's a very strange thing that she didn't mention it to me.'

'It just happened a couple of days ago, Mike. I finally managed to see her — and we talked.'

Michael thought about it for a moment. He studied Linc and asked, 'How long will it take? To drive?'

'Two, three days, the most,' said Linc. 'We'll be in Dallas by Monday. At the latest,' he added, almost apologetically. 'She doesn't go into surgery till Wednesday morning.'

But Linc's efforts at trying to appease the boy were a waste of time. Michael snapped, 'And you think you can make up ten years in two or three days?' His voice crackled with accusation. The brittle bite in his voice delivered the question in the manner of a prosecuting attorney. Linc felt the sting of Michael's question. It was obvious from Linc's voice that the boy had wounded him with the accusation. Linc's answer was barely audible. He said, 'I can start, Michael.'

Michael's eyes blinked, considering the answer. Resigned for the moment, he turned away. Reconsidering his options, the boy turned and looked at Colonel Davis.

'Sir,' he said, 'is my grandfather aware of this change of plans?'

Colonel Davis looked at the boy. Then slowly and deliberately he said, 'I'm leaving for the airport immediately. I intend to tell him personally.'

'Yes, sir,' the boy said, saluting the colonel sharply. The colonel returned the salute. Then the boy turned and walked out the door.

The colonel's eyes shifted to Linc.

'Thank you, sir,' said Linc, exiting after the boy.

24

With true concern in his voice, the colonel said, 'Good luck, Mr. Hawks.'

When Michael saw the truck and trailer parked in front of the school, he couldn't believe it. The idea of traveling alone with his father all the way to Texas was bad enough, but the shock of seeing what Linc was driving was truly revolting to him.

'We're going in *that?*' exclaimed Michael with disgust.

But Linc fielded the question with a good-natured smile.

'Slickest rig on the road,' he said. With Michael's bag in his hand, Linc climbed up onto the rig. He slipped into the cab and eased himself into the sleeper area.

He squeezed in behind the seats and stowed Michael's bag in a small closet. After an afternoon of playing peek-aboo with the clouds, the sun broke through, sending a shaft of bright light into the sleeper through the domed skylight in the roof.

But the skylight was only one of several features that Linc had installed in the rig. The most impressive, and for him the most beneficial, was the gymnasium equipment built into the trailer.

On the wall hung a streamer announcing the reason for the gym equipment. The streamer read: 'World Arm-Wrestling Championship — Las Vagas, Nevada.'

It was there that Lincoln Hawks intended to make all his dreams come true. Las Vegas was the final leg of his mission, and winning the world arm-wrestling championship would complete the assignment, fulfill his dreams, and at last set him free.

Far below the arm-wrestling streamer hung a color picture of a fleet of shiny, new trucks. Lincoln Hawks intended to one day be the owner of such a fleet — a trucking business he would call his own. It would be his kingdom, his domain.

For many people Linc's dream was a foolish exercise in futility. The idea of a trucker winning the world arm-wrestling championship was childish enough, but the notion that he could bankroll his winnings into a bundle to found his own trucking empire sounded to some of his friends like nothing more than the energetic chatterings of a little boy in a man's body.

Most men put away such foolish ideas when they finally realized how the real world worked. It was a steady grind, nine to five, day by day. At some point — usually upon finishing school or following their discharge from military service — most men ceased to play the game of dreaming faraway dreams of championships. That kind of life was reserved for the rare birds who became youthful million-aires by playing professional sports, making movies, or singing rock and roll. This might be America, where any-thing was possible, but it was still foolish, pathetic really, to be a grown man with a wife and a son and at Linc's age to still be chasing a dream. And what made it worse was that Linc made no bones about it. He was rolling everything on the dream, every penny he'd saved, every dime he could borrow and if necessary everything he owned. He'd worked, planned practised, lived, and dreamed his mission impossible.

It was a three-parter: one, he would get his son back, two, he would win the World Arm-Wrestling Championship, three, with the money won arm wrestling, he would buy his fleet of trucks — and a company he would run with his son.

But as Linc slid open the door on the cab of the truck and looked down at the young, scornful face staring up at him, he knew he still had a long way to go on the first leg of his plan. Forget two and three for the moment. He might physically be reunited with the boy, but he knew he was a long way from having his son back.

It was only in extending his hand down to offer the kid a lift into the truck that he noticed that the boy wasn't even looking at him. He was intently watching Colonel Davis' VMI station wagon easing out of the parking lot.

Linc turned and saw the wagon spin off in the direction of the airport. He looked down at the boy. Michael turned his eyes from the station wagon to his father. He saw Linc looking down at him. An understanding smile spread across Linc's face. He offered his hand to help him up into the truck. The boy accepted neither hand nor smile.

He said, 'No, thank you, sir. I'm quite able to manage on my own.'

Linc's lips tightened. He nodded agreement and stepped back to watch the climb. He had to admire the little punk. Even with his frail body and snotty attitude, the kid had spunk. He had no idea how to climb into the cab of the truck, and he could find nothing to hold on to to pull himself up. The steps were too high for him to reach, but some way — after skinning his shin and dirtying his pants leg — he climbed into the truck. It had been a root-hot-or-die performance of determination, but he did it. He shut the door behind him, took a deep breath with his back to Linc, to get his wind back, then turned and dropped himself into the passenger seat beside his father. The same matter-of-fact, business-as-usual blankness covered his face as he sat down. He never looked directly at Linc.

Instead, he stared directly ahead, looking out the windshield. Linc looked at him quizzically. He was an interesting kid, and Linc's feelings about him were mixed. He was amused by his gritty performance getting in the truck, but there was something about his stubborn determination that Linc liked. But for Linc it was quite understandable. Michael was his son. He had to be stubborn and determined. It was in his blood.

'Ready to roll?' asked Linc, flipping switches to bring the big turbo unit humming to life.

The boy turned and looked at him. His eyes were hard and shiny as tiny black marbles.

'Do I have a choice?' he asked.

Linc ignored the question. Instead he continued his preheat ritual with the rig, rattling off information and explanations like a guide at Disneyland.

'What we have here is an air-suspended cab with a double bunk right behind these fully adjustable seats. Plenty of room back there — even have a skylight. See it?' he asked, pointing to the dome in the roof.

Michael nodded that he could see it. He wasn't impressed with skylights.

Linc continued his good-natured pitch, undaunted by his son's coolness. 'And all my gym equipment.' He waited to see if there was a response to that. Maybe a question. Nothing. He continued, 'Air conditioning, full carpeting . . . dual armrests . . . state-of-the-art dashboard . . . a Cobra 21 GTL CB . . . a fuzz buster . . . AM-FM with dual speakers . . .' As he introduced the sound system, he popped a tape into the machine and hit the controls. The unmistakable voice of Willie Nelson flooded the cab. The deadpan boredom on Michael's face dissolved into a twisted wince of displeasure. He stared at Linc but said nothing, his eyes narrowing into slits.

The big engine started to chug and belch and roar with power. Linc started his series of forward gear shifts. Slowly guiding the thirteen-geared big baby through her paces, taking his time as she rumbled to life.

'Yes, sir,' he said, raising his voice over the increasing noise of Willie Nelson and the big engine coming to life, 'chrome bumpers, West Coast mirrors, stainless-steel quarter fenders —'

'Sir,' said Michael, interrupting him sharply, 'it isn't

necessary to make conversation for my sake. I can go for days without speaking.'

Linc smiled and, looking at him, said, 'You must have Indian blood in you.'

Immediately, the boy snapped, 'I am *not* Indian!'

Turning the steering wheel and wheeling the rig out into traffic, Linc answered him good-naturedly, 'I've always considered myself spiritually an Indian — a Comanche. And you and I look kinda Indian . . . and Hawks sounds like an Indian mane.'

'But my name is Cutler,' replied the boy.

Linc leveled the truck out onto the highway leaving the school. He settled back into his seat and, without looking at the boy, said, 'You shouldn't look down on people for bein' what they are. There's nothin' wrong with bein' an Indian — or a trucker either.' He turned and looked at Michael. The look on the boy's face did not indicate pride.

Michael turned and looked at his father. A snide curl formed at the corner of his mouth. 'You drive a truck because you're too stupid to do anything else,' He spat back at Linc.

The words hit Linc in the face like a slap with a wet towel. He turned his eyes from the highway and stared at the angry-faced boy beside him. The boy turned back to the highway, leaving Linc the tight-jawed profile of an angry, hostile stranger.

For ten years Linc had dreamed of being able to return to the son he'd been forced to leave behind. Now he was back — had the the boy with him. He was ready to fight for him and, if necessary, die for him. No cost would be too high, no battle too dangerous. But for what? What had they done to the boy? What kind of lies had been fed this kid to turn a twelve-year-old into an uptight, hostile, pain-in-the-ass robot spitting out someone else's programming?

He didn't know what kind of lies he'd been told, but Linc was sure of one thing. He knew the man behind the lies. He knew the liar. His name was Jason Cutler.

CHAPTER FOUR

Jason Cutler was not accustomed to losing. He was one of
the richest and most powerful men in the United States.
Rich and powerful men know many ways to keep from
losing. Jason Cutler knew them all. He knew a few that no
one else knew. He was a terrible loser. Even when he lost,
he did not lose. He had ways of reversing decisions to his
advantage.

After losing a zoning dispute that kept him from opera-
ting near a residential area, he carefully started buying the
entire neighborhood through surrogates. He continued the
buying until he owned every house on the 118-block
square. It took him three years to buy all the homes, but
when it was finished, he had no more residents to complain
against him. The zoning restriction was lifted. Cutler's
empire spread.

Sixty-two years old, he was a trim, hard, combative man
who showed no signs of age except for a head of silver-
white hair. He was a rugged, vigorous man who had been
born in one of Texas' poorest counties and raised in one of
its poorest families. But like hearty Texans before and
after him, he left poverty and suffering behind him by
wheeling and dealing his way into the good graces of the
state's power brokers.

From Texas wildcatter to southwestern cattleman to
Sunbelt real estate magnate, Cutler rode the commercial
whirlwind to riches. His private fortune was estimated by

Forbes to be in excess of one and one-half billion dollars. His ventures had turned a wildcat oilman into a multi-national conglomerate. But billionaire or not, he was still nothing more than a wily shit-kicker putting the squeeze on those who could make the sweetwaters flow in his direction. He had been fighting from the time he was a dusty ragtag Texas kid, and he still liked a good dirty fight even more than he enjoyed gobbling up corporations.

A good fight made his heart beat with excitement. It was his idea of fun.

He had learned early that the best way to win fights was to use all the tricks you knew. Some people called them dirty tricks. Some called them illegal. But Cutler came to realize that those were only words that meant something if you were stupid. The game was not won by playing hard or fair. The game was won by playing smart. Jason Cutler played smart.

At age eleven he had watched his father, a shade-tree mechanic, who had busted his fingers working in garages all over the county, stand arguing with the wealthy rancher who owned the car his father had repaired. Cutler's father argued his case and stood up for the integrity of his work and refused to release the car until he had been paid. The rancher stopped arguing and reached in his hip pocket for his wallet and handed over a fifty-dollar bill to the greasy mechanic. The rancher laughed and said, 'Son of a bitch, it ain't nothing but money.' He took the keys to the car, tipped his hat to the mechanic, and drove off smiling.

Two weeks later, the mechanic was found sprawled in the back end of a pickup at the wrecking yard. He had been beaten so badly by the three men who jumped him that he was never able to work on cars again. He repaired lawnmowers and died coughing up blood because he was too proud to take charity and couldn't pay for a doctor.

The rancher was elected to the hospital board, and when

he died in an unexplained automobile accident many years later, his picture appeared on the front page of the local paper, along with the listing of his many contributions to the community.

Jason Cutler never forgot the incident. Jason Cutler forgot very little. If there was any chance an incident or event might be used one day to his benefit, he stored it away, like a squirrel preparing for winter.

He expected those who worked for him to be as wily and resourceful and hard-nosed as their boss. If they couldn't cut it, he didn't need them.

Life was tough, and he said he'd heard all the sad stories he wanted to hear in country music. He couldn't stand listening to the shit, but sometimes a little familiarity with it came in handy.

To say that Jason Cutler was calculating would minimize the man's devotion to business.

He had once given thought to becoming governor — not running for the office, that was considered a formality — but becoming governor. But after calculating what it meant, he dismissed the whole idea at a meeting with his supporters in Houston. He told the roomful of rich backers and political hatchet men, 'Piss on it. The job's too small.'

Jason had everything he wanted — everything he could buy or steal. He even had a beautiful daughter and a grandson for an heir. Why in hell would he want to be governor?

When Colonel Davis reached the county airport, Jason Cutler's jet was parked on the tarmac. The colonel was greeted by Tim Salenger, Cutler's personal secretary.

Salenger was a preppy young executive in his early thirties with straight blond hair parted on the right to cover his receding hairline. The rawboned young man had grown up in Oklahoma and gone away to school in the East. He'd graduated from Princeton and received his law

33

degree at Duke.

He had been working for the Sierra Club, representing them in a case against one of Cutler's subsidiary companies, when Cutler noticed the young man. He impressed Cutler in court with his colorful preparation and command of the facts. The case was thrown out of court after three days, but not before Cutler sent word to the young man that he'd like to meet with him.

The morning after the dismissal of the case, Cutler and Tim had breakfast. That night Tim left for Argentina to represent the Cutler empire in a labor problem in South America.

'Good to see you, Colonel,' said Tim, opening the door of the colonel's car.

'Thank you,' said the colonel as the two men shook hands.

Davis looked over his shoulder and saw Jason Cutler coming down the steps of the plane. Behind him was another man, slightly younger than Tim but much taller and more powerfully built. He was Cutler's personal bodyguard and trainer. Cutler was never seen without the man. He answered only to the name Ruker. Little was known about him, and there was something about him that made most people uneasy. No one was sure what it was. His skin was olive smooth, and his hair and eyes were very dark. They seemed to match the man's sinister presence. It was well-known that Ruker was one of the very few Caucasians ever to be awarded a master's rating by the Japanese Aikido Association in Tokyo. He was a swift, supple killer, a man who knew many ways to kill — most of them with his hands.

'Cutler looks upset,' said the colonel.

'Yes, sir,' said Tim.

The two watched Cutler stride hurriedly toward them.

'Bad news travels fast,' said the colonel.

'Yes, sir,' said Tim.

'Where's Michael?' barked Cutler, dismissing the pleasantries of a greeting. However, he did stick out a hand and pump the colonel's right arm as he continued with his questioning. 'What happened? I got word that he'd been called back just as he was about to leave in the limo.'

'That's right,' said the colonel. 'I sent for him.'

'So? Let's have it. Where is he? What's the problem? Let's get it straightened out.'

The colonel relaxed his posture and said, 'There's no problem. Michael's fine. He's with his father.'

A slow, menacing frown broke over Cutler's face. 'What do you mean?'

'The boy left the school with his father.'

The muscles stiffened in Cutler's neck. Tension spread across his back. His eyes locked on Davis. Behind Cutler, Ruker remained ominous and foreboding as ever, like a force from the unknown, emotionless and uncaring. Tim's eyes darted back and forth between the two men, shifting his weight occasionally from foot to foot and tilting his head away from the wind while smoothing his hair down with his hand.

Cutler bit the words off slowly: 'You'd better explain, Colonel. I'm not reading you.'

'The boy's natural father — Lincoln Hawks — arrived at the school to pick him up. He had proper identification as well as additional proof he'd brought along.'

Gritting his teeth, Cutler whipped his head away from the colonel. He growled epithets to the wind, 'Goddamn, son of a bitch! Good God, man! I specifically called you yesterday and made a special point of saying that if that son of a bitch showed up, you were under no circumstances to allow him to see or speak to Michael!'

'Granted, sir,' said the colonel. 'The boy's mother called, Mr. Cutler. She insisted that Michael leave with his father.'

that Michael leave with her father.'

'Dammit, Davis, you know she's in no condition to make that kind of decision. She's dying!' He squinted his eyes, and the cords in his neck tightened. Deliberately and slowly, he said, 'My daughter is back home in Texas — *dying*. You have one conversation with her, and in spite of everything I told you, you turn my grandson over to that conniving, worthless bastard who deserted them before Michael was even two years old.'

The colonel hesitated for a moment. Cutler's presence was beginning to unnerve him. He was well aware of Cutler's power and influence, and was now trying desperately to recover lost ground. He tried to keep his words slow and measured, but failed as he stammered out a reply.

'But Mr. Cutler,' he said, 'your daugher was particularly lucid today. As a matter of fact,' he continued, 'when I questioned her about her state of mind, she put her doctor on the phone to reassure me that she is in full possession of all her faculties.'

Stunned by the statement, Cutler felt betrayed. It was as though he had been personally double-crossed, not only by his own daughter, but also by her physician — the best heart specialist in Texas, and therefore in the whole goddamn world.

Blood pumped to his temples, making the veins pulsate. It was obvious to Davis that he had surprised Cutler. Before Cutler could recover and reply with a question, the colonel offered one himself.

'Shall I tell you exactly what she said?'

'No,' snapped Cutler. 'Goddamn you. I by God don't want to know.' He waved his hand and turned away. 'It doesn't matter.' He turned back and eyed Davis. 'You understand? It by God doesn't goddamn matter.'

The colonel did not move. His eyes stayed on the man spitting out fury and frustration. Then a most surprising thing happened. A calmness started to settle over Cutler. It was as though a cloud of some kind of magic dust had fallen on him, transforming him completely. His body relaxed and the rigid anger in his face melted into a slow-breaking smile. It was a disarming, shit-kicking, good-ole-boy Texas grin. It was a tactic the clever bastard had used so many times he had it down to perfection. This mercurial quality of being able to quickly deceive and confuse partners and adversaries had made him millions. This chameleonlike ability to appear one way and then suddenly appear to be the exact opposite was his greatest gift.

'No hard feelings,' he said. He sighed, hitched his pants, and added, 'Given the same cards, I'd have played 'em the same way.' It was a lie, of course, but he could always come up with the most believable readings. A lie detector would have been no match for Jason Cutler. He believed what he said. Even when he knew what he was saying was a lie.

He turned to Tim Salenger and in a very friendly, business-like manner said, 'Tim, I want a check for two million dollars on the colonel's desk by this time tomorrow.'

'*Two?*' asked Tim. 'Not *one?*'

The colonel could not believe his ears either. He didn't know what to make of it. But he said nothing. He watched Cutler respond to Tim's question. Cutler rubbed his cheek with his fingers, as if checking to see if he'd shaved close enough. He slipped his hands into his pants pockets and rocked back on the heels of his Luccase eel-skin boots and said, 'I believe I said *two*, didn't I?'

Tim nodded almost apologetically, flashing penitence in his eyes. Cutler stepped to the side and looked at Ruker. 'Sensei. Did you hear me say two?'

'Very clearly,' said Ruker. His voice was deep and damp and dirty.

'That's right,' said Cutler.

'Thank you, sir,' said the colonel.

Cutler gave the colonel a quick, friendly smile and said, 'It took a lot of spunk for you to come out here. Face me down on this when you knew exactly how I feel about the boy.' Cutler rubbed his palms together and dipped his head downward, almost as if he were shooting dice at a crap table. His eyes rose from the ground and settled on Davis. He was smiling that cowboys-and-farmers-can-be-friends smile again. He chuckled and said, 'Hell, you had to know that you might blow that million-dollar endowment I've been dangling in front of you for a year.'

Regaining his courage, the colonel said, 'It was a risk I had to take.'

Cutler arched his eyebrows and looked at Ruker. He was still smiling. Ruker was not. 'Well, you see,' he said, addressing it almost to Ruker and Tim, 'brass balls pay off.' Tim smiled. Ruker did not. Neither did the colonel. 'I just upped the ante to *two* mil.' He paused for a moment and then said to the colonel, 'Turn it into a library — in Michael's name. Deal?'

Smiling like a jackass eating briars, he held out his hand to the colonel. The colonel shook it.

'Thank you, Mr. Cutler. It's very generous of you.'

'My pleasure. Just teach my grandson the kind of courage you brought out here to face me.'

'I'll do my best, sir.'

The colonel turned and climbed back into his car and pulled away. He waved good-buy to the smiling Cutler, but as the car made its swing and turned away to leave the airport, Cutler's smile slowly began to erode. The calculating eyes squeezed down tightly on the exiting station wagon. Then he turned and focused the hard, questioning eyes on Tim.

'I thought Hawks' truck was supposed to break down before he reached here.'

Tim shrugged as the three men started to walk toward the plane. 'I guess he drove in earlier than we expected. The junkman must have missed the connection.'

'No shit,' said Cutler. 'Pretty sloppy work, Tim. Pretty sloppy.'

'You might remember, sir.' said Tim very defensively, 'that nobody knew that Hawks was going to be in this part of the country until just a few hours ago.'

'That's right,' said Cutler, pausing on his climb up the steps to the plane. Turning back, he looked down on Tim. 'But that dosen't seem too demanding to me. Is the job getting too demanding, Tim? You want me to handle this one myself?'

'No, sir,' said Tim. 'It won't happen again.'

Cutler smiled at him and very fatherly said, 'I know it won't.' Then he winked at Tim. 'By the way, I want Davis fired.'

On the highway adjacent to the airport, Linc and Michael were heading for Texas. In the cab of the truck, Willie Nelson continued to wail.

'Sir,' said Michael.

Linc glanced at him and said, 'Yo.'

'We gotta do something about that,' he said rather distressfully.

'What's that?'

'That,' said Michael, jabbing a thumb at the speakers.

'Whatta ya mean?' asked Linc, cutting an eye toward the speakers.

'The music.'

'You don't like music?'

Michael sighed. 'I don't like cow-hick music.'

Linc's head snapped as if he'd been punched in the nose. 'Cow-hick music,' he said. 'That's Willie Nelson.'

'I know who it is. I don't like it. In fact, I *hate* that cow-hick stuff.'

Still unable to believe the heresy, Linc said, 'C'mon, everybody likes Willie Nelson.'

'I don't,' said Michael flatly. 'And I would greatly appreciate it if you would *turn it off*.'

'Sure,' said Linc, trying not to be offended. 'But this particular song I've sorta adopted as my theme song. It's an old standard, but it sorta captures my feelings.' Then to illustrate for his son, Linc began to sing along in his husky garage-basement baritone.

Linc turned and glanced at his son to see what he thought of the sentiments. Michael sat in stony silence, staring down the road at the planes taking off from the airport.

Linc wrinkled his nose and shrugged. He punched the reject button on the machine and caught the Willie Nelson tape in his hand. He slipped it into the tape rack and said, 'Okay. So whatta ya wanna hear?'

'Nothing, sir. Just nothing at all.'

'Come on. Whatta ya like? Tell me what ya like. We'll play that. I got some of everything.'

Michael turned and with frost coating the words said, 'I doubt that.'

Boastfully, Linc said, 'Go ahead. Try me.'

'Talking Heads,' said Michael.

'Umm. New group?'

'Power Station.'

Linc started to answer. Then he realized that the boy was being deliberately cruel to emphasize their differences. Linc got the message — not only was there a personal estrangement, there was also a cultural gulf between them. Instead of answering, Linc swallowed his words and eased back in his seat.

Michael turned away, gloating. He was particularly proud of his triumph. For he had demonstrated with rapier precision on Father Strange the peril of trying to get chummy with him.

But as he looked out of the window of the truck, Michael saw something at the airport that took his attention. He could see his grandfather's jet taxiing down the runway for takeoff.

Instantly he yelled out, 'I'm sick. If you don't stop quickly, I'm going to throw up all over the truck.'

'Hold on,' said Linc with concern. He hit the air brakes. He slowed the rig and brought it to a slow rolling stop.

Almost before the truck stopped rolling, Linc jumped from the cab and raced around to the other side to help Michael. But before he could get there, Michael threw the door open and leaped from the truck and dashed across the highway.

Linc saw the tiny figure running aimlessly into the path of the oncoming traffic. Horrified at the sight, Linc bolted after the boy.

Dodging the cars in the highway, Linc could hear Michael yelling, 'Grandpa! Grandpa, don't leave me.'

Running as fast as his legs would carry him, Linc streaked toward his son, causing a speeding Camaro to hit the breaks hard. The car skidded and squealed and fishtailed out of control. Behind the Camaro, the driver of a Dodge Dart could do nothing but slam on the brakes and fight the steering wheel and try to avoid the crazy kid and wild man charging across the highway.

Linc's speed overtook the boy, and with one quick powerful swoop of his arm, he had the boy safely in his grasp. The Camaro skidded past them, narrowly missing Linc. Following his momentum, he took the boy with him in a roll onto the shoulder of the road and out of the path of the careering Dodge Dart.

On the ground Linc held the boy tightly in his grasp. His heart pounded with mule-kicking force against his chest.

41

He struggled for breath.

Michael shivered in his arms, writhing with anger and frustration. Amid the gasps for breath, Linc said, 'It's all right . . . It's all right.'

From the highway horns were blaring and curses were being yelled. But Linc ignored the highway noise. He was only concerned with the unhappiness coming from the lips of the boy in his arms.

'He flew off,' sobbed the boy. 'He flew off and left me.'

'Who? What are you talking about?' asked Linc.

As Linc released the death-grip hug he held on the boy, Michael pulled away and scorched Linc with the most hateful, unforgiving eyes he had ever seen. '*I hate you*,' snarled his son.

The boy had landed another precision clean punch. The words struck Linc like a hammer. But he took the remark gamely. Reacting with a stunned smile, he pushed himself up off the ground.

'I'll accept that for now, Mike. It's better than no feeling.' He pulled the boy to his feet and reminded him, 'I told you, we gotta start somewhere.'

But as they started back toward the truck, they encountered one of the irate drivers who had come back to share her thoughts with them. A frazzled yuppie in designer jeans and high heels and silk blouse yelled out, 'What the fuck's the matter with you? You trying to get us all killed?'

Linc grinned and held his son's hand tightly. 'Me?' he asked. 'Try to get someone killed on the happiest day of my life? I don't know what you're talking about.'

Then he walked away, leading Michael across the traffic-free highway.

Behind him he could hear the woman talking to two men, but he didn't bother to look back.

*

For several minutes Linc drove in silence. Thoughts were rushing through his mind on everything — his wife, the boy, the grandfather, memories of the years he'd been away from the boy. But he knew it was too late now. He couldn't worry about what might have been or should have been. It would help nothing now to second-guess his decisions. It was past history. He remembered what he'd heard a football coach say to the team after getting beat 44 — 0. The coach had said, 'Anybody that worries about what happened yesterday is stupid. It's over. Look to tomorrow. Because there's not a damn thing you can do about yesterday.' Linc remembered the occasion and half smiled just thinking about it. But he knew then and he knew now that the coach was right. There wasn's a damn thing he could do about what had already happened.

He glanced over at the present sitting beside him. The uncommunicative boy sitting next to him in full military uniform with the stiff chin-high collar — that was the present. That was what he had to deal with — the morose kid staring out the window. Maybe he could still connect with the kid, he thought. He had to. He couldn't just wait for him to like him. There wasn't time.

'Why don't you get comfortable, Mike? Loosen that collar for a start. You can't be comfortable all buttoned up like that. Let your skin breathe.'

'I'm fine, thank you sir.'

I'm fine, thank you, sir. Thank you, sir. No, sir. Yes, sir, rattled through Linc's head. This kid's a machine, thought Linc. I'm his father and I get answers like he was talking to the President.

'You want a Coke?' asked Linc. 'Or a Seven-Up? There's a built-in ice chest just behind your seat.'

'I don't do soft drinks.'

'Only the hard stuff, huh?' said Linc with a grin.

But the boy did not bother to dignify Linc's attempt to

lighten the tension between them. He refused to show even the trace of a smile. He just stared out the window, looking at the billboards flying past them.

Undaunted, Linc continued to make suggestions to the kid. He was trying his best to strike life into the zombie son that sat staring bleakly out the window, watching the world rush by.

'There's a map in that compartment in front of you. Hand it to me. I'll show you where we are,'

'I'm quite familiar with where we are,' said Michael. 'At the moment we're about twenty miles north of Lynchburg.'

'Right on,' said Linc, gesturing at him with a tight fist. 'Couple of more hours we'll be rolling across Tennesee. I know a great little stop for Kansas City beef — just before the state line. They truck it in every day from K.C. — seven hundred and twenty-three miles — best T-bone in the Southwest.'

'I don't eat red meat.'

Linc couldn't believe it. A boy twelve years old who didn't eat meat!

'How do you expect to grow up?' asked Linc with genuine concern.

'It's against my religion.'

'What?' yelped Linc. 'What religion?' he asked in disbelief. 'You got some religion I don't know about?'

'Good health,' said Michael.

'Do I look like I'm wasting away?'

Michael didn't answer him. He didn't turn to look at him.

Linc sighed and considered for a moment. Then he announced sternly, 'Look at me!'

The boy turned, and with the same blank expression and vacuous eyes, he looked at the muscular, rugged Comanche wheeling the rig down the highway.

'So whatta you see?' asked Linc, his voice cracking with

emotion. 'A victim of bad health from eating red meat? Is that what you see?'

The hood slid back on the boy's eyes, and looking at Linc with boredom, he said with a condescending whine, 'Later in life it'll catch up with you.'

'Grab hold of that handle,' said Linc firmly.

'What handle?'

Linc pointed to the handle on the dashboard attached to the flex-steel and rubber cords. The boy did not wish to play the man's silly game, but because of Linc's commanding presence and the firmness of the command, he took the handle in his hand.

'Pull it toward you till your fingers touch your chest,' explained Linc.

The boy pulled on the handle. The compressed cords barely responded. He couldn't budge the cords. In frustration he dropped the handle.

Linc grabbed the handle and flexed it easily to his chest. The muscles bulged like shaped steel on his powerful arm. His bicep swelled large and hard, a large smooth stone balanced on the bone.

'Red meat,' said Linc triumphantly. Then he snapped the exercise device back and forth several times. It was if there were no tension on the cords at all as he pumped the springs back and forth repeatedly.

As he continued to pump the machine, he said, 'Red meat's what you need to build muscles like mine. You don't get these kindda arms from eating bean sprouts.'

'Everyone knows red meat has been linked to heart disease and some forms of cancer,' Michael replied condescendingly.

Like a linebacker pumped for action and angry with frustration, Linc continued to rattle the machine with action. It was as though the dashboard might explode and shatter as Linc jerked the handle again and again to his chest.

Even Michael, for the first time, seemed concerned. The violent physical display of power and passion had in some way penetrated the boy's cool exterior. But Linc did not notice the slight admission of curiosity in Michael's eyes. He was fiercely exercising and driving the truck at the same time. He couldn't study the reaction of his spectators too.

He continued to pump his strong right arm until sweat started to appear on his forehead above the headband.

But as he continued to rip away at the exerciser, Michael stared at something other than the highway. He stared at the strange creature that was his father.

When Linc began to cool down, he eased the handle back into place. He caught his breath by sucking in air and blowing it out. Then he patted at the sweat on his forehead with the back of his arm.

'Boy,' he said. 'Worked up a sweat.' He glanced over at Michael, but the boy quickly diverted his eyes back to the highway.

'Just talking about steak gets my juices going,' he joked, trying to lighten the moment. But the boy had retreated again into the billboards and scenery.

Linc said, 'You'll like Martha's place — that's the truck stop I was telling you about before. Some of the best truckers in the world'll go hundreds of miles out of their way to get a sample of her cookin'. She makes the best steaks you'll find in the whole country. And I know 'cause I must have tried them all.'

Michael curled his lip. 'Sounds like a great place to line your arteries with cholesterol. I'll bet she puts salt on everything, too. That's a major contributing factor in high blood pressure.'

'Say what you like but I've been living on country fried

steaks my whole life. You may think my kinda diet'll make you sickly, but I know hundreds of truckers who'll prove you wrong. Just wait till we get to Martha's — you'll see what I mean.'

Linc glanced over at him. He shook his head slightly and returned his eyes to the road. For several miles they drove in silence, without music or conversation. They listened to the engine hum and watched the highway whirl by.

It was late afternoon when Linc wheeled the Silver Hawk into Martha's Truck Stop Diner's parking area. Just the sight of the diner's sign seemed to relax his growling stomach.

Several truckers in the parking lot and a couple at the diesel pumps waved to Linc as he maneuvered the big rig through the parked trucks.

'Those are today's cowboys,' said Linc, nodding his head toward the truckers.

'If those truck drivers are the cowboys, are you the token Indian?' asked Michael snidely.

Linc grinned and replied cheerfully, 'Nope. I'm an Indian cowboy.'

Michael groaned. 'Sure,' he said.

'You know how much those men drive in a week? Some of 'em drive as much as twenty-five hundred miles. They haul everything — zinc, asbestos, perfume, records, beer, bricks. It don't matter.'

'Sure a lot of trucks,' said Michael as they continued to move among the rigs.

'Yep,' said Linc, starting to name each truck as he spotted it: 'Freighliner . . . GMC Astro . . . Kenworth W900 . . . Ford LTL 900 . . .Mark Cruise Liner . . . International Eagle Brougham Conventional . . .'

'Okay, okay,' said Michael.

'One more. See that? Diamond Reo with a Cummins

four-hundred-horsepower engine. Baby will rumble. You know something else?' asked Linc.

'What?'

'The men that drive them are just as different as the trucks they drive.'

'They all look the same to me — baseball caps and blue jeans.'

'That's where you're wrong.'

Linc eased the rig past the gas pumps and brought it to a stop out of everyone's way. But before he opened the cab door, he turned to his son.

'All right,' he said. 'No steak for you. Fine. Bertha makes a great fried chicken. Now, don't tell me you don't like fried chicken. Every American boy likes fried chicken.'

'I'm not hungry,' said the boy.

'Right,' Linc said with frustration. 'You're not hungry. All right, how about coming in to use the john? You haven't asked for a pit stop since I picked you up.'

Michael didn't bother to hide his disgust. He curled his lip and snarled, 'I can just imagine how clean their rest room is.'

Linc, a little surprised by the remark, said, 'Bertha's bathrooms? Cleaner than at home.'

The boy did not intend to check it out. He wanted no part of the hairy-chested, low-rent world he saw on parade outside the diner.

'I'll stay here, sir, if you don't mind. You go eat your red meat.'

Linc scratched his cheekbone and rubbed his nose, staring into the distance. He was thinking just how to approach this kid without blowing his cool and making things worse.

Very softly he asked, 'Look, what is it with you? You won't loosen your collar. You won't eat. You won't even take a piss!' He relaxed, licked his lips, and came at the

48

boy again, trying with all his heart to woo the kid out of the truck.

Entreating the boy to join him, he said, as one buddy to another, 'Hey, Mike, come on, huh? I gotta go. I also gotta eat. I gotta build my strength for what's coming up next week — most important week of my life. And yours too.' He paused and waited for a response. When none came, he playfully waved his hand in front of the boy's face.

'Am I getting through to you?'

The boy sighed, pursed his lips, and said, 'I don't understand a word you're saying.' Then the boy added, almost pleading his request, 'Can't you please, sir, just go do what you have to do?'

'I can't leave you out here by yourself.'

'What if I promise not to run away?'

'That's not the problem,' explained Linc. 'I leave you out here your grandfather will swoop down like a bald eagle and grab you away.'

The image seemed to please the boy. Pleasure shone in his eyes.

'You're afraid of him, aren't you?'

'Yeah,' said Linc with unconcern. 'Afraid of what I might do to him.' Then he shifted the tone in his voice and demanded. 'Now — are you coming or not?'

The boy did not quickly respond. He thought about it. His dark eyes scanned the lot and then shifted to Linc.

'Can this Martha *broil* the chicken — leave off all the guck?'

'Why not?' shrugged Linc. Grinning, he said, 'Who wants all that good-tasting guck anyway?'

Linc opened the door and climbed down. On the passenger side Michael managed to do the same.

When Michael entered the diner with Linc, the boy knew his evaluation of the place had been right on target. It was cow-hick city.

The boy's feeling that the place was just a congregating place for the Middle America machismo crowd was what Martha's was all about.

The place was packed with beefy hard-nosed, hard-driving, hard-living cowboys of the highways. To Michael, they were cow hicks. Same as the music. Low-life losers. They looked ignorant and dirty, and he knew they'd just as soon break his neck as spit on him.

But the boy was not intimidated. He stood ramrod straight in his uniform and paid no attention to the truckers slapping Linc on the shoulder, or the ones yelling their greetings to him from across the room.

Linc wanted to take the boy by the hand and yell out to the room, Hey, look at this. My kid. I got him back. But he knew better. Still, the beam on Linc's face said what he didn't dare say out loud.

One thing the boy was quick to note, however, was that that despite the roomful of men with bulging biceps and trunklike necks, most of the hulks seemed to have some kind of special respect, admiration, or something, for his father.

As they moved from booth to booth and table to table in the din of noise, it appeared to Michael that the men were waiting for his father — anticipating his arrival. It didn't make sense to the boy, but nothing had made sense to him since he entered Colonel Davis' office.

Martha's was a home away from home for the truckers. It was a place for them to let their hair down and blow off steam, boast and bullshit, eat good food and drink beer. The place was an outpost, a convention hall, a clubhouse for the men who made the highways hum.

Martha's was an enormous room of booths and tables. There was a bar for those wanting liquor.

Waitresses in white uniforms carrying armloads of blue-plate specials played the truckers like harps and went home with purseloads of tips. Country music played full blast day and night.

Martha's was the place to be, but Michael didn't want to be there.

In the corner of the dining room sat a huge mountain man named Bull Hurley. He was different from the other men in two respects: One, he was bigger than anyone in the room. He was a giant, almost inhuman in dimension. The second thing that made him different was his intense interest in Linc. He did not glad-hand or yell. He sat quietly, just watching.

Sitting at the table with Hurley was a man named Earl Landis. Landis was Hurley's manager. Bull Hurley was the world champion of arm wrestling, and he had come to Martha's for no other purpose than to see for himself this arm-wrestling trucker that he had been hearing about. Bull Hurley took his arm wrestling seriously. That's why he was world champion. In his opinion championships were lost because of slothfulness and overconfidence. He entertained neither. He worked hard, trained hard, and kept his mind on his business — the competition.

Landis leaned across the table and said, 'I told you. Man's got nothing. You can tear his head off.'

Hurley diverted his eyes away from Lincoln Hawks and eyed the little man in the tweed jacket across the table from him for a second.

'Shut up,' said Hurley in a voice as soft and pure as an angel's breath.

Landis said nothing. He decided to enjoy the Kansas City steak that Martha was famous for. He quickly went to work with his knife and fork.

Hurley's attention turned again to the man standing beside the boy in uniform.

*

Linc found the two men he had waved to at the gas pumps, and he and Michael joined them at their table.

They shook Michael's hand and told him how great it was to meet him, but they couldn't restrain themselves any longer and quickly shifted the conversation to the subject that had them so excited.

Ken, a tall dark-haired man in a brown-and-yellow plaid work shirt, leaned in close to Linc and whispered, 'Have we got a live one for you today.'

The other man, shorter and built like a tank, wore his rusty-colored hair cropped just short of an old-fashioned crew cut. But no one ever saw it. He wore his CAT 'gimme' cap day and night, in the house and outside as well. With his red hair and blockbuster body, it was no accident everybody called him Brick.

'He heard you were comin' through, so he hung around since yesterday — that's how hungry *he* is,' explained Brick.

'Dumb bastard really thinks he can take you,' snickered Ken.

'And he's got a stash he's willing to bet,' added Brick excitedly.

Linc considered the news and asked, 'You seen him in action?'

'Only his mouth,' said Ken.

'He's so hot to trot he's even willing to give odds.'

This rarity piqued Linc's interest. Impressed by the man's confidence, Linc said, 'Man must be good, huh?'

Ken said, 'Hey, Linc, you wanna eat first or put him outta his misery?'

Linc turned to Ken and cocked his head and said, 'Little exercise never hurt a man — especially before dinner. Bring him over.'

Ken and Brick jumped from their seats and hurried away to find the eager opponent. In their hurry to get away, they all but ran over the owner of the diner — Martha herself. Brick and Ken grabbed the tiny gray-haired woman and did a Texas two-step with her to break their momentum.

'Whee,' squealed Martha.

'Whoa,' yelled Brick, holding the woman and dancing in place.

'Sorry, Martha,' said Brick. 'Didn't mean to run you down.'

'What in the world's the big hurry?' asked Martha.

'We got a pigeon wanting to test Linc,' said Ken.

'Oh, my,' exclaimed Martha.

'Don't worry,' said Ken. 'Nothing's gonna happen.'

'Just bring you more business,' said Brick. 'That's all.'

'Yeah,' said Martha, disbelieving and moving away from the boys. 'Well, let me talk to him before you boys start that mess.'

'Go right ahead,' said Brick, and the men hurried away on their search to find their arm wrestler.

'So this is your boy,' exclaimed Martha, approaching the table.

Linc smiled proudly and said, 'Twelve this week.'

'Looks just like you, Linc,' said Martha.

'Michael, this is the famous steak lady — Martha —'

'Just Martha,' she said.

'How do you do, ma'am,' said Michael courteously.

'Such a wonderful birthday present seeing your father again.'

Michael glanced at Linc. Linc took a deep breath, preparing for the boy's retort. But to his surprise the boy showed his class. Like the good VMI cadet that he was, he didn't make a smart-aleck remark to the woman. He respected her as a woman and recognized his duty to his elders. He replied in the courteous manner that had been bred into him. He said, 'It's been a real surprise, ma'am.'

Linc sighed and looked across the table at Michael. He

53

was grateful.

'Well, you two have a lot to catch up on, so I'll leave you. Your usual two T-bones, Linc?'

'Right,' said Linc with a wink.

'How about a nice dinner steak for Michael?' asked Martha.

Quickly Linc answered, Mike feels like chicken to-night, Martha.'

'Wonderful,' exclaimed Martha. 'Nice and brown?'

Linc wrinkled his face as if he were working on the decision and suggested, 'Broiled. Not fried.'

Martha reacted with surprise. She looked askance at the boy.

'Not fried?' she asked.

Michael shook his head and said, 'I'd like some cold milk to drink.'

'Make that two milks,' said Linc.

This really took Martha by surprise.

'What?' she squawked. 'No Bud six-pack?'

With a gesture of open arms and complete surrender, Linc begged, 'What? I'm in training?'

Martha shook her head and tousled Mike's hair. The boy didn't like it and made no attempt to hide his displeasure at her try for intimacy. But Martha didn't notice his grimace. She smiled at Linc and shuffled off to put their orders in the works.

Linc smiled across the table at Michael and said, 'That was Martha.'

Michael didn't reply. His eyes drifted away from the table. Linc turned to see what it was that had attracted Michael's attention. He saw Brick and Ken moving toward him. A monstrous human hulk walked along with them. The size of the man alone took Michael's breath away. The giant was easily six-seven and had to weigh three hundred pounds at least — most of it in his massive chest, shoulders, and arms. He stood at the table looming over Linc and Michael like a giant redwood. In the monsters's mouth was the chewed stub of a cigar, which he puffed and shifted about in his mouth while blowing smoke across the table at Linc. Through a cloud of smoke he said, 'You Silver Hawk?'

Very amicably, Linc said, 'Yeah.'

'I'm the Smasher,' said the cigar-chomping tree. 'Heard you calling Smoky earlier today when you were out on 305. Real wipe-out, huh?'

'Pretty bad,' said Linc.

'Know who the trucker was?'

Linc shook his head.

'Word around here is that he was Texan.'

'Drove like it.'

With that, Smasher swallowed the cigar butt. The bug-eyed Michael couldn't believe what he'd just witnessed. His eyes remained glued on the giant, expecting smoke to shoot from the man's ears. Instead, the man went right on talking as if nothing had happened.

'Well now, looka here. Silver Hawk, how'd you like to wrestle me?'

Linc looked him up and down and scratched his shoulder and neck and considered it.

'I don't know. Maybe we oughta wait till we meet in Vegas, huh?'

'What's a matter? I got too much weight for you? Outta your class?'

'Hey, man,' begged Linc, 'I been driving for hours. I just ordered my steaks. My boy here is hungry. Gimme a break, huh?'

Brick and Ken exchanged glances and kept straight faces, revealing nothing.

Smasher growled, 'All I been hearing lately on the road is Silver Hawk, Silver Hawk, Silver Hawk — he's the dude to beat.'

Linc dismissed the talk with a shrug. 'Just some of my rowdy buddies talking big.'

The Smasher threw two fingers down on the table, pressing firmly, 'Two out of three, okay?' he asked, pushing for the match.

Linc rubbed his stomach and looked across the room, ignoring the Smasher.

'Make it just one. One's okay.'

A slow grin spread across the Smasher's face. Triumphant, he looked at the eager-eyed Ken and Brick. Behind them truckers were beginning to sniff the makings of a match.

'It's on,' said Brick.

Immediately, wallets and cash started to appear. Bets began to be made, then Smasher proudly announced to the crowd, 'I'm laying a thou on myself.'

'At what odds?' asked Ken.

Pulling a huge roll of bills from his red wool jacket, the Smasher yelled, 'Five to one, I'm one — he's five.'

The odds gave those hesitating all the stimulus they needed. From booths and tables the truckers began to dig into their pockets for cash. Everyone wanted to get in on a match with five-to-one odds.

Michael remained confused. He still hadn't recovered from Smasher's swallowing the cigar butt, and now the betting and boasting, yelling, and general mayhem around Michael made the boy feel as if he'd fallen into the middle of some kind of midway freak show.

Men crowded around Linc, loking him over as if he were a piece of meat or a prize bull ready to be auctioned. But Linc seemed to enjoy it, smiling and nodding and flexing his bicep good-naturedly.

Neither Linc nor Michael, nor for that matter, anyone else noticed the mountainous Bull Hurley move through the crowd for a closer look at Lincoln Hawks — the Silver Hawk.

He pushed his way past some of the toughest truckers on earth without as much as an angry word being said to him. He wanted the best vantage point possible for the match, but he didn't want to get too close to Linc. He didn't want to reveal himself. He wanted to be an unnoticed observer.

Hurley's tiny tweed-coated manager hopped along behind his monstrous champion, like a remora tagging after a great white shark.

He squeezed in beside Hurley, and through his tortoise-shell-framed glasses he watched the last of the bets being laid down on the match.

Brick held cash in both fists and continued to grab a few more as he yelled, 'Last chance to get your money down. Silver Hawk versus the Smasher.' He held up one finger from the huge wad of bills in his right hand and explained, 'One touch only.'

The Smasher wiped at his nose with the knuckles of his right hand and sat down opposite Linc. The eagerness in his eyes was evident. He exercised his fingers as he opened and closed his fist several times for Linc's benefit. But he was wasting his time. Linc had already checked out.

Michael watched his father suddenly transform himself into something the boy did not understand. Linc had retreated into a private world of pure crystalline concentration. He had moved to another plane of existence. His arm was already on the table. His forearm was erect, his fingers and palm open. He was ready and waiting for the gods to touch him with power.

The Smasher smirked at the demonstration of concentration and stared hard into Linc's eyes, which had turned into mysterious dark black pools. Unable to penetrate Linc's private world, the Smasher chuckled, dismissing the concentration as another wrestler's gimmick.

He placed his elbow on the table and lifted his hand

opposite Linc's waiting palm.

Brick and Ken stood between them, acting as judges. Brick squatted down and lined himself up with the two contestants' upraised hands. He raised his right hand as if he were about to signal the start of a road race.

In open-mouthed bewilderment Michael saw his father's hand enveloped by the Smasher's huge paw. But despite the size of Smasher's giant hand, the two arms remained locked in place, rooted to the table at the elbows. Immediately, the men began to jockey for position. Each man moved to take the advantage. The Smasher called upon his massive size for strength and pushed against the resisting power of Linc's arm. However, where the Smasher seemed to be exerting himself, Linc appeared relaxed, passive, almost bored. Linc was holding his own, but the Smasher felt nothing threatening his strength.

Confidently, he turned his head to the ring of cheering trucker faces and boasted, 'He ain't got it.'

Brick quickly jumped into the fray and adjusted the placement of the two men's arms, but the supremely confident Smasher snarled at Linc, 'Gonna drop you on the table, Silver Hawk. Be nothin' left but feathers after I break off your arm.'

'Are you ready?' asked Brick, his eyes darting back and forth between the wrestlers. Then he adjusted their arms once more, making sure they were aligned and ready. He raised his arm again, paused for a second, studied the two men, and then after a three-second interval he brought down his arm. With the downward thrust of the arm came the command: 'Go!'

At the sound of the word 'go,' the seemingly transfixed, meditating Linc suddenly came to life. His entire body became a gigantic locked spring. He was an overpowering, truning, whirling torque, turning like an unstoppable transmission. The powerful right arm stood strong and erect, like a steel beam. It was the unflexing extension of the powerful body's torque. The giant arm of the Smasher began to tremble and slowly give way to Linc's crushing arm strength. The Smasher's arm tilted backward, moving closer and closer to the tabletop.

As the Smasher's arm gave way, the men with bets riding on the giant screamed for him to resist. Meanwhile, Linc's red-faced supporters squeezed their fists tighter and tighter and begged for Linc to put him down. In the center of this cheering, gesturing hurricane of activity stood the perfectly passive and restrained Bull Hurley. Only Hurley's eyes moved, shrewd, calculating eyes that registered every minute move made by Lincoln Hawks.

At the urging of his fans and supporters, the Smasher began to call upon hidden reserves of strength in his huge body. But as Smasher made this final surge to overpower Linc's advantage, an electrified burst of energy exploded from Linc. With a remarkable lightning-bolt blast of power, he slammed the Smasher's arm fiercely to the table, smashing the arm through the tabletop.

With his arm caught in the splintered wooden table and totally exhausted by the physically draining battle with Linc, the Smasher collapsed headfirst onto the table.

Like a surfer being swallowed up by a giant wave, Linc disappeared in the whooping and hollering ocean of fans. The Smasher's friends quickly moved in to try and rescue their wrestler from the table holding him a prisoner. With his arm pulled loose from the table, the woozy warrior rose to his feet and was led away. Meanwhile, Ken and Brick stuffed their pockets with money.

Bull Hurley remained unmoved and motionless. He stood perfectly still, considering what he had just seen. Seeing that his man seemed troubled by the match, Landis decided to reassure the champ. He said, 'You can take that sucker with your pinkie.'

Hurley glanced at the little man trying his best to be helpful. 'Shut up.' he said. Then he turned his thoughtful attention back to the Silver Hawk, who had come out of his trance and was accepting the hurrahs of his near-delirious friends. He grinned a happy-faced grin at Michael and said, 'Surprised, huh?'

Michael remained speechless. He couldn't really believe what he had just seen with his own eyes. Linc leaned down near his son and in a low voice said, 'That's what's gonna get me my fleet.'

'What fleet?' asked Michael.

But before Linc could explain, Ken and Brick crowded around Linc's table and dumped wads of cash onto the table. Together the men counted out one thousand dollars and shoved the cash toward Linc. Linc took the bills and folded them without bothering to check the count. Then he shoved the folded bills into his jeans pocket.

'Did you have to break the table?' demanded Martha, pushing her way up to Linc.

Linc turned away and pointed to Ken and Brick. 'The boys here'll settle up with you on that, Martha.'

'You kidding?' chirped Martha. 'Nobody touches this table. Truckers will come for miles around just to see where you creamed the Smasher.'

Linc grinned, and Martha explained, 'I just wanted to tell you that your orders are almost ready — five more minutes.'

'We sure could use that milk.'

Martha slapped Linc on the shoulder and flashed him an 'okay' signal with her thumb and index finger and headed out for the kitchen.

Linc smiled and turned back to Michael, but before he could get a word out a trucker shouted to him over the the celebrating crowd.

'Linc! A couple of assholes are outside messin' around

60

your rig.'

'Know 'em?'

'Watch the kid,' said Linc, turning to Ken and Brick.

They nodded, but Linc was already on his way to the door. The crowd shifted like a tidal wave toward the windows. The first to arrive was Michael. He pushed up close to the glass and stared out toward the trucks. At Linc's truck he saw two tough-looking dudes slashing at the tires with knives. Then he saw his father running toward them.

The man Linc reached first was bent over tearing at the wheel with the knife. Linc was on him before the unsuspecting man could even come to his feet. Linc drove his elbow down into the man's neck and shoulder. The man crumpled face first into the dirt.

At the sound of Linc's attack, the man's accomplice, a bigger man wearing a blue-jean jacket and sock cap, leaped in front of Linc and took a swipe at him with the knife.

Linc easily sidestepped the flick of the knife and grabbed the man's outstretched arm. Immediately, he wrapped his left arm under the man's pinned outstretched arm and gripped his own left wrist with his other hand. He heaved his body back and up. The leverage against the man's trapped arm was too much for the bone. The elbow disconnected.

The man screamed in agony and staggered away, holding the limp spaghetti string that he been his arm.

However, from the shadows of the rig, five men began to move in on Linc. In their hands Linc could see weapons — tire irons and clubs. But instead of retreating, Linc charged the men, dropping the lead man with a straight back kick into the man's lower stomach. The man dropped the tire iron and fell to his knees, holding his belly. Kneeling, he was a sitting duck for Linc's spin kick. Linc's boot caught the man at the jaw, almost taking his head off.

61

The destruction of the attacker was thorough and complete, but it was a foolish mistake by a seasoned brawler such as Linc. Turning his back to the men allowed them the split seconds they needed to rush him. The four fell on him like blitzing linebackers. Linc's knees buckled, and he staggered backward, collapsing under the weight of the four men.

At the sight of Linc falling under the four attackers, Brick and Ken bolted for the door of the diner, followed by Michael and several truckers.

With the attackers on top of Linc, he started to use his knees and elbows to defend himself and keep the brutes off him. However, in the process Linc was taking a lot of blows himself.

A tire iron crashed down across his back, and pain stabbed up his spine and into his shoulders. In quick retaliation he grabbed a frizzy-topped goon by the hair and pulled him close to his face. Then, like a mad dog he savagely clamped down with his teeth on the man's ear. The man screamed as the ripping pain shot into his brain. He kicked and danced, screaming for freedom. But like a bulldog, Linc would not release his bite. In desperation, the man pulled away, tearing flesh to free himself from Linc's grasp. Blood dripped through the man's hand as he fell away from the fight, holding his ear to his head.

Linc wanted to kill them all, tear their heads away, and he fought fiercely. A foot slammed into his stomach. He gasped and felt the hard iron of a tire tool strike his head. He collapsed as the electric explosion of pain surged through his body.

He could hear sounds — the grunts and groans and curses of the three men — but he could also hear the faint echo of a voice calling to him from the crowd.

It was Michael. He had broken from the crowd. The boy was pleading with the men to stop. As two of the men straightened Linc up against the truck, the third started to do business. The semiunconscious Linc felt only half the pain as the man teed off on Linc's head with his fists. Linc's head flopped from side to side with every wallop.

'Please! No! Stop!' screamed Michael. The thick-chested man in the blue jumper dishing out the punishment turned and looked at the screaming boy in the military uniform. He grinned and with his tongue licked the blood oozing from the side of his mouth. Then he turned and sent his fist crashing against Linc's cheek.

Michael turned to the crowd and screamed, 'I thought you were his friends! Help him!'

But before the men could respond or speak, everyone's eyes shifted back to the fight as Linc roared like a lion and with an incredible demonstration of strength, literally lifted the two men holding him off the ground and pitched them forward. But as they fell, they grabbed Linc by his sleeves and pulled him forward, toppling him down on top of them. With Linc on the ground, the third man clubbed Linc across the head and shoulders with the sawed-off fat end of a pool stick.

Blood dripped from above Linc's eye. He could barely see. He blinked and tried to focus. His brain was hazy. So was his ability to focus. But he could see something coming toward him. It was huge and moving relentlessly, like a train. He felt another slash of pain shoot through his head as the club whacked a chopping blow against his temple.

Then suddenly the massive moving train was on them. Bull Hurley turned the thug with the club and with a mighty swipe of his arm, he demolished the man like a grizzly knocking a human aside. Then he reached for the two remaining men holding Linc. He took a fistful of shirt in each hand and lifted the two men off the ground and walked with them to the truck. Their legs dangled trying to touch the ground. He held them up and away from him. He paused, stared at them for a second, and with no more effort than a kid splattering two eggs against a wall, he smashed the men's bodies against the truck. They hit the wall face forward, and Michael grimaced at the horrible sound of teeth and bone shattering. But instead of dropping the men, he smashed them against the truck, not once or even twice, but three times. It was as if he needed to complete the routine of a newly-created body building exercise. When he'd finished with them, he tossed the limp bodies aside as if they were disposable trash to be collected later.

Michael raced to Linc and knelt beside him. Linc pushed himself painfully up off the ground. He saw Michael's concerned face through the daze of blood and double vision. Tears streamed from the boy's eyes. Linc grunted with pain, and the boy sniffed, 'Just because I hate you, I don't want you to die. Please don't die!'

'Takes a hell of a lot more than a few punks with tire irons to finish off your old man,' said Ken, kneeling beside them. He took Linc's arm and whispered, 'C'mon now. Your steaks are on the table.'

Brick moved in and grabbed Linc on the other side. Together they brought Linc to his feet.

'Come on, Linc. You know Martha likes you to eat her food hot.'

Linc mumbled incoherently, and the two men walked-carried the groggy trucker toward the diner. Michael walked behind the men. The tears flowed freely from his eyes, but his fingers wiped away the tears as fast as any windshield wiper working against the rain.

The same as at any accident scene, the gawkers and on-lookers melted away as quickly as they had come. All except for two — the huge Bull Hurley and his bespectacled manager — stood watching Linc being carried into the diner.

'If you figure he's going to be any kind of competition, why'd you step in and help him?' asked Landis. 'And don't tell me to shut up,' he added tartly.

Hurley sighed and answered, 'If I explained it to you, you still wouldn't understand. So . . . shut up.'

They turned and walked away together toward a candy-apple-red Ford pickup. On the door panel was a reproduction of Dean's bulging right arm. Underneath the mighty arm was the legend: 'Bull Hurley, World Champion Arm Wrestler.'

Hurley opened the door and fell into the second seat, filling it completely. Landis slid in under the wheel, adjusted his glasses, and kicked off the engine. The glasspacks crackled and reverberated. Landis grinned, buckled his seat belt, and hit the gas. The red Ford truck spun out, throwing dirt at the door of Martha's diner.

CHAPTER FIVE

Inside the diner Linc ate his steak and Michael nibbled at the chicken.

'I feel better now,' said Linc, patting his tummy.

'Pardon me for saying so, sir, but you don't look so good.'

Linc grinned. 'These little old things,' he said, pointing to the cuts and scratches on his face. 'That's nothing. We gotta hit the road, ole buddy.'

'Do you really think that's best?'

'I think it's what we gotta do to get to Dallas,' said Linc, reaching for the dinner ticket.

Michael said nothing more. He walked stoically behind his father, receiving pats and good wishes from Linc's friends. When Linc paid for the meal, Martha tousled the boy's hair and slipped him a handful of bubble gum.

Michael said, 'Thank you'. and kept it in his hand until they were in the truck. Then he dumped it on the dashboard, where it stayed until Linc started chewing it.

As they rolled through the hills of Tennessee, Linc blew bubble-gum bubbles and Michael dozed with his head on the window. He jerked awake at the sound of a man's voice calling, 'Breaker, breaker . . . Roadmaster to Silver Hawk.'

Michael blinked and stared into the night. For a moment he didn't know where he was. Then he saw Linc reach for the CB microphone.

'Okay, you got the Silver Hawk here. Come back, Roadmaster.'

Michael sat up straight, still in the twilight of sleep but awake enough to be aware of the CB conversation.

Roadmaster's voice crackled through again on the radio. 'You know who that guy was you arm-wrestled at Martha's?'

'The Smasher,' replied Linc.

'I mean, do you know who he *really* is?'

'Guess not,' said Linc.

'Only the champion of all Canada,' chirped the Roadmaster's voice.

Michael turned and looked over toward his father. Without noticing the boy's interest, Linc replied, 'Hey, that's good. Those Canucks are almost as tough as us truckers.'

'The odds against you just dropped from a hundred to one to eighty to one. You know who else was at Martha's?'

'Who else?'

'The world champ — ole Bull Hurley himself.'

'Yeah. What was he doing there?'

'On his way to Vegas for the competition. But he made a special point of stopping off to size you up. You're looking good, Silver Hawk. Getting famous.'

'Yeah. I do seem to be attracting a lot of attention lately from all sorts of people. I'll catch you on the flip side, Roadmaster.'

'Ten-four. We gone.'

Linc hung the mike on its holder and blew a huge bubble.

'Sir . . .'

Linc popped a bubble and licked the gum back into his mouth. Playfully, he answered, 'My name's Lincoln. But in your case I'll make an exception. *You* can call be Linc.'

Not responding to the teasing of his father, Michael

68

asked seriously, 'You still claim you don't know who those men were?'

'What men?'

'The ones who tried to kill you,' said the boy, almost sternly.

'Just sore losers. Probably bet on the Smasher,' said Linc.

'A lot of men lost bets. *They* didn't try to crush your skull with tire irons.'

'Hey, that's a good point,' said Linc, registering the first serious consideration of what the attacks might mean. 'I wonder who those guys were?'

'Are you still dealing drugs, sir?' asked Michael, almost accusingly.

Linc splattered the bubble he was working on and turned toward the boy. In the dark cab he could only see the shadow of the boy's stern-serious face. At first Linc did not answer. The impact of the question stunned him, angered him. Finally he replied, 'You couldn't have thought that up all by yourself, could you, Mike?'

'My grandpa gave me the facts.'

'Grandpa sure covers all the bases, doesn't he? What facts?' demanded Linc.

'He said a tractor like this one costs close to a hundred thousand dollars — and a refrigerated trailer about thirty-five thousand. And he told me that when you met my mother you didn't have a nickel to your name. He says you didn't really go off to fight in Vietnam — that was just an excuse you used to leave us. He says all the years you were away in Asia you were making a fortune in drugs in the Golden Triangle. That's why you've come back and bought this truck — for your business.'

Linc could not believe his ears. For hours he'd been trying to get the boy to talk, and now, finally, the boy had said more than he had for the entire day. All of it garbage. Utter rubbish. As Linc sat at the wheel listening to the poison spill from his son's lips, he kept thinking to himself how gratifying it would be to see Jason Cutler standing on the highway ahead of him, trapped in the middle of the road.

Linc felt blind hate burning in his blood, making him want to scream angry denials at the pack of lies. But he knew that Cutler had used every kind of cheap deception to turn Michael against him. He also knew that screams and denials would only work against him. Even thoughtful explanations would not span the enormous gulf between him and Michael. He had to reach him some other way. He had to make the boy feel. He had to communicate to him *his* feelings. But how? he wondered. He turned and looked over at the boy. Linc was hurting, but there was no way for Michael to know how much. The boy simply stared back at his father. There was no forgiveness, no understanding anywhere in the boy's eyes.

It was hard to see clearly in the night, but Linc could see enough. He knew the look. He'd seen it before. He'd seen it all day long, and he'd seen it ten years before on the face of Jason Cutler. He was glad that it was night. The darkness muted the cruelty in Michael's eyes.

Not being an educated man, Linc reacted the only way he knew how — with action. Ahead of him he saw a turnoff he knew very well, and he swung the big rig toward it. The truck hit the side road at high speed. Linc wheeled the truck onto a dirt road, not bothering to slow down. He bounced the load into the Tennessee woodlands. Michael sat stiff as a stick, holding on to the door handle. He tried to ride steady, but the bumpy exit bounced him up and down on the seat like a tenderfoot in the saddle. He had no idea what his father was doing, he didn't dare ask. He intended to ride it out to the finish.

The tree limbs and low branches whipped against the Silver Hawk and made the boy flinch with every pop and slap of a limb against the roof of the truck.

As the truck cut its path through the woods, the light of the headlamps brought distant objects into view. Illuminated in the two beams of light was a broad, swift-flowing river. And the truck was rushing pell-mell toward the water.

The boy's muscles tightened. His lips were dry. He looked anxiously at his father's tight-jawed, determined profile. Then he looked quickly ahead of them and saw they were all but upon the river.

He was ready to scream when Linc hit the air. The powerful trailer and tractor shuddered and shook and ground to a halt only a few feet from the water's edge.

The boy exhaled and sat perfectly still. Linc killed the diesel. Neither man nor boy moved a muscle. Outside the truck they could hear the mighty river rumble past them. Linc still sat with his hands tightly gripping the steering wheel. He kept his eyes focused straight ahead on the star-spangled river shimmering with heaven's light.

Michael licked his lips and swallowed. His heart was pounding hard and fast. He turned to his father, and the aftershock tension of the rocky ride to the river exploded from his lips.

'*Shit* — Sir!'

To Linc's ears, the explosive curse was a long-awaited sign of humanity. He turned slowly toward the boy.

'Some crazy dope dealer, huh?' he said with a grin. 'That what you thought?'

The boy didn't think it very funny.

'I didn't know what to think,' he said.

'Yeah, I guess that's tough — not having Grandpa to tell you what to do,' said Linc. Then he turned and popped his door open and climbed out.

Michael glared at him, but he did not move from his seat. He watched the stranger outside the truck peel off his headband and unbutton his shirt.

'You know how to swim?' asked Linc, pulling off his shirt.

'Naturally,' said the boy stonily.

'Okay, then. Let's go,' yelled Linc.

Michael looked at the man slapping his hands together. Then he looked at the churning white water. 'In there?' he exclaimed.

'Where else?'

'I swim in pools, sir, not in dirty rivers.'

'Look, Mike,' said Linc, sitting down on the ground to pull off his boots, 'I'm hot — I'm mad — and I need to cool off! But I don't dare let you out of my sight.' he flipped his boots toward the cab and pulled off his socks. 'So climb down. Come out here on the bank where I can watch you.' he hopped to his feet and began peeling off his jeans. 'We're going to be camping here tonight anyway, so you might as well take off your uniform and wash some dust off.' Linc tossed his jeans on top of his boots and stood in his jockey shorts, hopping from foot to foot like a boxer loosening up before a bout.

Without replying, Michael opened the door on the other side of the cab and climbed down and crossed to his father. A look of incredulity creased his face. 'Camping,' he asked in disbelief, 'here? All night?'

'Yeah, all night. You don't like the trees maybe? The river? The moon?' said Linc, gesturing broadly with his arms to all of nature's scenic wonders. 'Is this too shabby — or what?'

'I assumed we'd be stopping at a hotel,' said the boy, 'where I'd have my own bathroom.'

'You got the whole outdoors for a john!'

'I'm not some animal! I don't go on a tree!' snapped Michael angrily.

'The tree doesn't mind. Why should you?'

72

'I need my privacy.'

'Look, when you gotta go, just tell me. You go south, I'll be looking north. You want to do it to the west, I'll look east. Now, is that fair enough?'

'Where do you expect me to sleep?'

Linc said reassuringly, 'Maybe you didn't see that big double bunk in the sleeper compartment. She's all yours. And I got some franks in the fridge. We'll make a fire and have a wienie roast.' Then, with a joyous, boyish whoop, he stripped off his shorts and plunged into the swiftly moving waters.

Michael stood motionless, stunned by the act. He watched his father swim into the raging river. It was as though this man were defiantly challenging the strong current. With strong, powerful strokes he cut through the water, demonstrating his power, showing the river who was boss.

Timidly, Michael moved toward the river. He seemed reluctant to approach the river, yet the performance of his father against the river's power seemed to lure him ever closer. It was as though the white waters shining under the moon and stars had cast a spell on him. As with Ulysses' wooing by the siren's song, Michael seemed unable to resist whatever it was that was calling him.

He sat down on a rock and removed the spit-shined, gleaming black dress shoes. He rolled off his socks and wiggled his toes. Then he rolled his trouser cuffs until they were up to about midshin, revealing his bare legs. He pivoted his body on the rock and lowered his feet into the water and let the churning white waters slosh over them.

He didn't want to admit it, but it felt good. He enjoyed it. It was pure pleasure. Encouraged by the powerful sensation, he decided to stand and feel the water at the edge of the bank. He very cautiously stepped toward a big flat rock resting in the river only a few feet away. He took a step toward the rock and placed one foot on the huge stone. Then he lifted his other foot to step out onto the huge rock. But his foot slipped on the slick moss on the stone.

Instantly he went down, splashing into the water as if he were a rock himself. Even before he could stand or climb to the rock, the swift-moving current snatched him away and took him rolling down river. For a second he went under, tumbling with the water's flow. Frightened and spluttering, he bobbed up out of the water, splashing and fighting. He thrashed about in the water as the river took him deeper into the surging water. At last, gasping and choking, he screamed, 'Help!'

Linc, who had momentarily forgotten about the moody kid — thinking he was still sulking on the bank — was having a fine old time cavorting in the middle of the river, doing his imitation of a salmon on its run. But at the sound of the thin, desperate voice calling for help, his eyes whipped back to the truck. The headlights of the truck were still shining brightly down on the river, but he did not see the boy. He was no longer on the bank.

He heard another scream for help. The call came unmistakably from downstream. With strong, powerful strokes Linc swam toward the scream. He could see the boy's arms shooting up out of the river, fighting at the churning, foamy water.

Linc began to cut through the water like an Olympic champion. Michael flopped helplessly about in the fast-flowing water. Then he felt something hard smack against his back as he bounced off a large boulder jutting up out of the river. Michael swirled on past the rock and down into the white water sluicing furiously at its base. Michael tried to resist the powerful force of the river, but he could do nothing except tumble headlong into the turbulence.

But even as the boy splashed into the water, Linc was

closing the gap, moving in on him as the boy's head popped up again, spitting water and gasping for air. Michael could hear a voice, like someone calling from far away in a dream. It was a shout: *'Keep your head up.'*

I . . . I . . . I . . . can't, thought the boy. I've been up . . . and up . . . and up . . . I can't stay up much longer.

Then suddenly the boy felt something whack at his arm and slide by. Something snagged his sleeve. Then for a moment he saw Linc's hand clutching at his sleeve. But as Linc struggled to bring the boy closer to him, another boulder cut between them, severing the two bodies. The only thing left in Linc's hand was the sleeve of Michael's uniform, ripped from the jacket's shoulder.

The raging water took Linc cascading downstream ahead of Michael, but as he rode the swift current, he saw a tree branch wedged between two boulders. Twisting and turning in the gushing water, he reached out and with a violent spasm of strength, he tore the tree limb free. With the aid of the branch, Linc moved toward Michael, thrusting it out as a lifeline to the boy.

'Grab it,' he shouted.

From the whirlpool of bubbling water, Michael lunged for the limb and grabbed it with both hands. Then, swimming with one arm and pulling Michael with the other, Linc began to tow the boy toward the shore. Fighting against the pounding force of the current, Linc pulled the tow limb until at last he found relief in a side eddy, where he pulled the boy, hanging on the limb, to him.

Then, swimming with an arm securely linked to his son, he hauled the boy onto the bank. He dumped Michael on the ground. Heaving for breath himself, he stood over the shaken boy. On his hands and knees Michael coughed and vomited up the river's water.

Kneeling beside Michael, Linc lifted the boy into his arms and held him. Gasping for air and coughing dry air, the boy fell against Linc, trembling like a baby bird. Linc wrapped his strong arms around the boy and hugged him tight.

With his strong right hand Linc tenderly pushed the boy's wet hair out of his eyes. He swept it back off his son's forehead and looked down at the face of the exhausted, helpless boy in his arms. He cradled his son in his arms and pressed the boy's head against his shoulder and started to rock Michael, like a mother rocking her baby to sleep.

Jason Cutler took the stairs two steps at a time, passing the giant crystal chandelier he'd shipped to Texas from France. He reached the second-floor landing of his Texas ranch house. He hurried down the hall toward a double door leading to his daughter's private wing. Outside the doors a doctor and nurse waited for him.

'She's been asking for you, Mr. Cutler,' said the doctor with concern.

Cutler did not bother to slow down or reply. He pushed past them and entered the wing occupied by his daughter.

He hurried past the library, the dining room, and the den and moved without hesitating into his daughter's oversized, lavish bedroom, which had been converted into a full-time hospital facility.

Electronic equipment, medical supplies, and oxygen tanks vied for space in the room with nurses and lab technicians, who moved about quietly doing their work.

In a silk-canopied bed lay Christina Cutler Hawks, a wasted, pale, almost ghostlike young woman. The woman was dying, and she knew it. The doctors knew it, and Cutler knew it. But he refused to admit it. For to face the inevitable truth meant that he — Jason Cutler — could not buy everything. The Cutler millions could not buy life. Death was easy. It came cheap. He bought it all the time.

But his first try at buying life was not going well.

He settled himself on the bed beside his still lovely daughter, leaned close to her, and kissed her on the forehead. He took her hand in his and held it, patting it gently.

'I had to fly from Virginia to New York. It took a lot longer than I thought it would. I just landed a few minutes ago. The doctor told me you were wanting to see me.'

Timid as a small girl, Christina asked, 'Are you mad at me?'

'Have I ever been mad at you?'

'Disappointed then?'

'You're my joy, sweet girl.'

'I defied you,' she said almost apologetically.

'Now, there I have to agree.'

'I never did before. In my whole life. But I did today.'

Jason faked a smile. 'Well . . .' he said, making light of it.

'Were you furious?'

'Right off, yeah. I was really pissed. But then I thought — what the hell. Maybe do the boy some good to see for himself what kind of a scumbag Hawks really is.'

'I have to tell you something, Papa.'

'Later, baby. Not now. Now you need to save all your strength for next week.'

'I'm going to die,' said the girl, with a frightening ring of certainty.

Visibly shaken by the remark, Cutler did his best to dismiss the comment with one of his good-ole-boy smiles. He shook his head no. But the girl's hollow eyes did not respond to his phoniness.

'They say you always know,' she said.

'Bullshit, honey,' snorted Cutler. 'You *never* know. What you're feeling — this . . . fear, this apprehension about . . . dying . . . that's all part of what happens to

77

anybody with a heart condition. It's only a symptom, like a headache or nausea. You understand? Just a goddamned symptom.'

'Well, it doesn't matter. That's not what I wanted to tell you.' She paused and considered what she'd say next. But knowing there was no way to ease into the revelation, she said it in one sentence, evenly and calmly: 'I've been seeing Linc.'

Cutler's eyes turned cold. He stared at his dying daughter.

'*Seeing* him?' he asked.

'Papa, I still love him,' she said. 'And Michael needs a father.'

'He has *me*,' said Cutler, biting the words off sharply. His jaw tightened, and he said nothing more.

Ignoring her father's comment, Christina said, 'If . . . I do get better . . . after the surgery, please promise me you'll give us another chance. Let Linc come back to us.'

'Just get well, baby,' said Cutler. Then he lied to the girl. He said, 'I'll give you anything you want. Even that son of a bitch!'

The emotionally dependent girl tried to say thank you by lifting his hand to her lips to kiss it. But the strain was too much for her. She dropped his hand and fell back in pain.

Startled by the reaction, Cutler waved to the nurses for assistance. Immediately, a nurse and a young intern hurried to Christina's side. Cutler rose slowly from the bed. He smiled a weak smile at his daughter and said, 'You just get some rest. I'll be in to see you a little later.' Then he turned and walked away. He was no longer smiling.

The gym was where Cutler took out his frustrations. Rather than smashing lamps and destroying tables, he turned the wild rage into a controlled weapon.

Still fuming from Christina's revelation that she and Linc had been seeing each other, Cutler backhanded a life-size dummy with vicious, almost maniacal fury.

He wore aikido gi with the stately-looking samurai black shirt and rear bustle. Again and again he tore into the dummy, relentlessly chopping, punching, and elbowing the throat area. The grim-faced Ruker stood behind him, somber as ever. He wore black stretch slacks and a black tight-fitting pullover. His arms were folded across his chest. When Cutler scored decisvely, Ruker nodded slightly to acknowledge his satisfaction.

Cutler continued to assault the lifeless form. In his mind he saw Lincoln Hawks, and he longed for the opportunity to personally tear the long-haired son of a bitch to bits. The sorry son of a bitch would never touch another Cutler, he thought as he smashed the dummy with a series of devasting combinations.

Still dressed in his business suit and street shoes, Tim Salenger strolled across the gym's polished hardwood floor. The sound of Salenger's clicking heels turned Ruker's head. But Cutler, deep in concentration, finished his attack. When he turned and saw him, he wasted no pleasantries on the young man. 'Well?' he demanded.

'You want the bottom line?' said the young man.

'Don't tell me he walked away this time?' said a disbelieving Cutler.

'From the report that came back he did,' said Salenger. Cutler's eyes cut Salenger like a razor. 'Yes, Sir,' said the secretary. 'He did.'

'*Seven* men?' said Cutler, seemingly dumbfounded by the news. 'And not a one of them could bring Michael home?' He turned away from Salenger. 'Jesus Christ!' he shouted, turning back to his secretary.

The younger man, with one hand in his trouser pocket,

explained, 'He got some unexpected help. Four of the men had to be hospitalized.'

'I hope to hell they've got Blue Cross, because I'm not paying one dime to the kind of bums *you* hire.' He glared at Salenger. The tension hung for an ugly moment. Then Cutler said with obvious sadistic delight in his voice, 'Take a trip, Tim. Go somewhere I can't find you. Call me in two weeks. I'll let you know if I ever want to see you again.'

In the Tennessee woodlands Michael Cutler prepared for sleep. He had settled into the big bunk inside the Silver Hawk. The boy wore white pajamas with antique cars on them. Linc stood beside him in a pair of dry shorts. In his hand was a sleeping bag. He walked to the door, paused, and said, 'You need anything, I'm right here,' motioning with the sleeping bag.

The boy nodded. 'Good thing I had these pajamas,' said Michael. 'Only dry things I have.'

'Aw,' shrugged the father, 'we'd a fixed ya up. I got plenty of stuff. Remember,' he added, 'ya need anything, just yell. I know ya can do that.' He grinned a good-natured grin, but the boy dropped his head to hide his embarrassment over his accident at the river. He nodded his head but still refused to look his father in the eyes.

Linc paused and wanted to say more but thought better of it. 'Good night, Mike,' he said lovingly.

The boy raised his eyes and said, 'Good night, sir.'

Linc smiled and closed the door gently behind him.

Linc walked down toward the river to the campfire he'd built after his ordeal in the water. He spread his sleeping bag beside the fire. Then he stepped to the other side of the fire to check Michael's clothing. The boy's shirt, trousers, and one-sleeved tunic all hung on a scaffolding of branches he'd built to dry the clothes. Linc touched the clothes to his hand. They were still wet, but he hoped that by morning they'd be dry enough for the boy to wear again. He squatted beside the fire and felt its cozy warmth on his body. It felt good. He rested an elbow on his knee and held his head in his hand and tried to make sense of the topsy-turvy roller-coaster ride he'd been on all day. After a few moments of thought, he rose and pulled his arms back, stretching the muscles in his back. He touched his toes with his hands a few times and gently rocked his upper body from side to side while holding his hips and legs steady. When he'd finished the light loosening exercises, he slid into the sleeping bag and peeled off his shorts. Lying inside the sleeping bag, he gazed out across the river. It was still beautiful to him, despite its attempt to steal the thing he loved most in the world.

As the river rolled by, humming its midnight lullaby, Linc wondered if the river had in some mysterious way given his boy back to him. Not just physically, but emotionally, maybe spiritually.

Linc had a feeling that the river and the rescue had in some way saved the boy — purified him. Salvation by water. He couldn't explain why he felt it, but he felt it in his heart. Sensed it.

The moon played hide-and-seek with the clouds. The river serenaded the stars. The frogs croaked to the Silver Hawk. He listened and smiled, then closed his eyes and was welcomed to the world of slumber. Lincoln Hawks was sleeping.

Michael Cutler was not. He threw back the covers on the bunk and crept along the floor to the wall of photographs. He knelt before them and studied them. The picture of Lincoln Hawk and Christina Cutler on their wedding day held his attention for a long time. Then his eyes moved on to look at the baby pictures.

He sat on the floor, gazing at the wall of photographs. He could not rationalize what he'd been told about his father with the shrine he'd created to his wife and son. The contradiction troubled him greatly. He had been told by his grandfather that Linc was a loser, a worthless piece of trash best forgotten. But the photographs suggested something different. The photographs troubled him. If his mother and grandfather had eliminated his father from their lives — and everything Michael had been taught to believe was true — where did he get the pictures? The boy was baffled.

Until now life had been laid out for him, and his grandfather had provided him all the answers. Anything that disturbed him was taken care of by his grandfather. And the boy's natural gifts, along with his rare backup system of tutors and special educational advantages, had made school easy for him. But this was different. The computer system couldn't kick out an answer; the Cutler millions couldn't smooth this one out for him. It was something he was going to have to wrestle with himself, and he was not used to wrestling with weighty problems. The problems he had faced usually went away. But this little dilemma was sticking with him.

The boy eased himself down to the far end of the bunk so he could look closely at the photos and posters on the bulkhead. The poster at the center was of two huge muscular arms locked in arm-wrestling combat. It announced the upcoming World Arm-Wrestling Championship competition in Las Vegas, Nevada.

Right below the arm-wrestling poster was an enlarged color photo of a long row of glistening new trucks, shining like diamonds in the sun.

Michael stared at the posters and pictures for several minutes. Then he crept to the window and peered out. The pensive young face stared down at the man sleeping beside the campfire's flickering flames. The boy's face was long and lonesome.

*

By morning the fire was only ashes, and Linc was sleeping the restful sleep of a man with a clean conscience. Then, suddenly, his eyes popped open. He stared straight up and saw Michael standing over him. Behind the boy he could see the sun bleeding through the trees as it made its morning move toward higher ground.

'Why did you leave us?' demanded the boy.

Linc rubbed his eyes and reached for his shorts with the other hand. He slipped his legs into the shorts and eased his upper body out of the sleeping bag as he sat up.

'You have any idea how you'll be seven years from now?' he asked.

'I don't understand what *that's* got to do with my question,' said the boy.

'Seven years from now you'll be nineteen. You'll still be wet behind the ears, even though you'll con yourself into believing you're already a man.'

There was nothing in the boy's face to indicate he understood. He simply stood staring blank-faced at his father.

Linc pushed himself up out of the sleeping bag and began pulling on his jeans. 'Well, I'd just turned nineteen when I married your mother.' He stood up straight and zipped the pants and continued, 'Like you say, not a quarter to my name — a high-school dropout, a real nightmare for your grandfather.

Michael did not move. He stood, arms folded, saying with his body language: convince me. So Linc continued with his attempt to make the boy understand.

'He made it impossible for your mother — and Christina's never been strong enough to fight him back,' he interjected. 'He turned against her, against me — just like he turned you against me.'

He turned his back on the boy and walked toward the river making the boy follow him.

'We lasted a couple of years, but I saw it was destroying her — trying to choose between me and her father. So just before you turned two I signed up for Nam. While I was still in the country, the divorce papers came through. So I took off, went to sea — merchant marine.'

Linc knelt down and looked across the river. The sun was just beginning to bounce its rays off the water. For a moment Linc said nothing. He seemed to be remembering the days at sea as he stared at the sun shining on the water. Then he said very softly, 'I saw the world, Michael. I learned there was nothing out there that meant more to me than you and your mother. So I saved every cent — and now I've come back to get my family together. I bought this rig and I had a good summer. Made forty-six hundred bucks for one run from Salinas to New York. Peaches from Georgia brought in another two. Bing cherries from Washington state scored me a big four grand. That's the kind of drugs I been hauling, Mike — celery and bell peppers and bing cherries.'

He turned and looked at the sour-faced kid, slipped his hands into the back pockets of his jeans, and continued, 'So over the years, lifting and hauling — I built my body, and to see who'd pay for the beers I started arm wrestling in bars all over Asia. Hey, I found out I was pretty good at it. So when I heard about this big contest in Vegas, I said to myself, that's it. I got an eighty-grand equity in this rig — and a real serious buyer waiting in Denver. You heard what the Roadmaster said last night I figure the odds'll drop some when word gets around but I'll still be a heavy underdog. The prize money plus what I can make bettin' on myself will give me a fair stake towards ownin' that fleet.

'The picture in the cab?' asked Mike.

'Yeah, ain't they beauties? They're the finest machines made in this country. When you drive those babies, you're goin' in style.'

Linc's eyes were flashing with excitement just thinking about the trucks.

'They're almost within reach, Mike,' he exclaimed. 'Once I'm over the top, I'm on my way!'

'*Almost* within reach,' repeated Michael sardonically.

The sarcasm registered with Linc, but he continued on as if he didn't recognize the nastiness. 'It's been a long uphill fight — but next weekend, Mike, it's over the top!'

'Grandpa's right,' snapped the boy.

Surprised by the remark, Linc lashed out almost instinctively. Not able to control himself, he whacked the boy's face with his open hand. Staggered by the blow, Michael fell backward but managed to keep himself from going down. Blood bubbled up on his lip. He touched the blood with his tongue and stared at his father. His eyes were hot and angry.

Linc moved to the boy, full of remorse and alarm. He wanted to hug the boy and ask for forgiveness. He wanted to apologize, but he didn't. He did nothing.

'I'd like to go home, please, sir,' said Michael stiffly. 'You promised me we'd be in by Monday morning.'

'We will,' said Linc, too quickly. Relaxing, he said, 'Get dressed.' Then he added almost inaudibly, 'I gotta work out.'

The boy turned and walked away, carrying his dry clothes in his arms. Linc watched the slender boy in pajamas with old cars on them climb back into the trailer. He puffed his cheeks and blew out the air in disappointment at himself.

Then, almost as if to compensate for his performance with Michael, Linc ripped into his exercise routine. With incredible vigor he began a routine of jumping jacks, push-ups, sit-ups, and body-stretching exercises. Finishing those, he moved quickly into a series of strength-building exercises devised to use his surroundings. He walked to the riverbank and stuck his fingertips into the hard-packed wet sand, pushing and pulling against his weight, building the strength in his fingers and hands. He waded into the river and lifted rocks and tossed them, curled them, held them over his head, and lowered and raised them again and again.

Then he lifted himself from the water by pulling himself up on a low tree limb, using it for a chinning bar. After chinning himself several times, he held himself up to the limb and hooked his chin over the limb of the tree. With only the strength of his neck and jaw, he held himself there. Then, using only one hand, he lowered himself back to the water.

In the trailer Michael looked at himself in the tunic with one sleeve missing. It seemed silly to wear a uniform with an arm completely ripped away, but he had nothing else to wear.

The boy said nothing when his father entered the compartment and went to work on the exercise equipment in the trailer. Linc's body glistened with sweat as he worked the various parts of his upper body on the springs and pullys designed to shape his chest and shoulders and build his awesome arms even more. Michael watched silently. In his heart he respected the man for his stamina, strength, and determination. But being a body beautiful was not enough to claim him for a father.

When Linc finished his exercises, he peeled off his jeans and jumped from the trailer and ran to the river and dove into the water. After swimming and relaxing for a few minutes in the cool water, Linc waded to the bank and toweled himself off and slipped into his clothes.

Michael stood silently watching him. Both hands were in his trousers pockets and he gave the appearance of someone waiting impatiently for a bus. It bothered Linc, but he continued to dress quietly. Finally he said, 'Why don't you take off that jacket?'

The boy did not move. The hands remained thrust downward in his pockets.

'You can't walk around with one sleeve,' said his father.

'I don't intend to 'walk around,' sir. I'm planning on our driving straight through to Dallas.'

'Wouldn't count on it. I said Monday morning. It's only Saturday morning now,' said Linc, reaching up and grasping the sleeve of Michael's tunic. He gave a quick jerk and ripped the arm of the jacket away from the stitching at the shoulder. He flipped the sleeve up onto the branch of a tree and said, 'Now it balances.'

It was obvious that the boy wanted to retaliate, but he knew there was no way. It would have to wait. He glared at Linc for a second, then turned and marched to the truck and climbed inside. With a violent closing of the cab door, he showed his father how he felt.

Linc ignored it all. He walked over to the truck and went about his routine morning inspection of the rig. As he checked the exposed running gear, he spotted a loose pigtail between the cab and trailer. He stopped and tightened it. He checked the tires and circled the rig one last time. Then he climbed inside the cab. It was highway time.

As they powered their way across the beautiful Tennessee hills, the boy asked, 'May I turn on the radio, sir?'

'Sure,' said Linc.

The boy snapped on the radio and started twisting the selector knob. Everywhere he rested the selection bar, he heard country music. Johnny Paycheck. Bobby Bare. George Strait. The Kendalls. The Oak Ridge Boys. Dolly Parton. Anne Murray. It didn't matter. It was all country.

Amused at the boy's inability to find any other kind

of music, he said, 'You're not going to find Talking Heads anywhere in the vicinity of Nashville.'

Peeved, Michael snapped off the radio. Still amused, Linc half grinned as they rode along side by side in stony silence.

Finally Michael broke the ice with a question. 'Would you like to know how *I* know that long, sad story you laid on me is a crock?'

'Yeah, I'd like to know.'

'You say that all the time you were gone you were thinking there was nothing else out there but Mama and me. Isn't that what you said?'

'Damn right,' chimed Linc.

'Ten years — just thinking about *us*, right?'

'Right.'

Then with a savage hiss in his shrill little voice, the boy asked, 'Then how come in all those years you never sent me a single birthday card or letter or *any*thing?'

Linc looked at the boy, bewildered by the question. 'What are you saying to me?'

Ignoring Linc's response, Michael continued, 'Not that I expected anything — or even wanted to hear from you. I'd have torn it up if you *had* sent it. But actions speak louder than words. We never once heard from you.'

Talking not so much to the boy as to himself, Linc said, 'Son of a bitch! I shoulda figured! Don't you see, Mike, that miserable bastard tore them up as fast as I mailed 'em in.'

'Blame it on him.'

'Goddamn right,' roared Linc. 'I wrote you a letter every day — seven days a week. Some were long, some were just 'Hi, kid.' But I shared every thought, every adventure I went through. It was like a diary, only instead of keeping it, I mailed it to you. Don't tell me not one got through.'

'Remind me to show you my scrapbook. Under the section marked 'Father,' there's *zilch*,' said the boy tartly.

'None of the presents either?' asked Linc. 'The stuffed kangaroo from Sydney? The giant clam shell from Tonga?'

'Sure,' piped Michael. 'Along with the elephant from Kenya.' Linc cut his eyes over at the boy.

'How'd you manage to get those snapshots of me — the ones you got on the wall in back.'

'How the hell do you think? Your mother sent them to me.'

'Why?'

'When we see her, we'll ask her,' said Linc cryptically. 'Okay?'

Michael frowned. He still didn't understand. He couldn't make sense out of it yet. But he was beginning to wonder if his mother had told him everything. He wondered if his mother really had secretly been in touch with his father. But any more thought about the question vanished when Linc said, 'Uh-oh. Trouble.'

Michael looked at his father. Linc was studying his side-view mirror.

'We've suddenly got a highway patrol car closing in on us.'

'Look,' said Michael.

'I see,' said Linc.

Down the highway ahead of them two Tennessee State patrol cars were blocking the highway.

'What's going on, sir?'

'I wish I knew,' said Linc, slowing his speed. He leaned over and opened the glove compartment and fished out his packet of permits, licenses, and registration papers. The squad car closing in on them pulled alongside, and the driver motioned for Linc to pull over.

Linc eased the rig onto the shoulder of the road and brought it to a stop a few yards from the parked cars blocking their path.

As Linc climbed down from the rig, six troopers in the three cars spilled out and converged on him. One of the troopers held a German shepherd on a leash.

'Who gets these?' asked Linc, holding up his packet of papers.

The officer who had been pursuing, a slim, dark-haired middle-aged man with a rakish mustache, took the packet without answering him. The other men formed a semicircle around Linc. He smiled at them awkwardly. They gave him nothing in return.

'Pretty good-size delegation. Somebody break out of prison or what?'

The officer glancing through the papers asked, 'Lincoln Hawks?'

'Yes, sir.'

'Who's the minor up there in the cab?'

'My son.'

'Please ask him to step down.'

Linc turned and motioned to the boy. 'Mike, come on down.'

As Linc continued to wait, shuffling his feet and sticking his hands in and out of his pockets, Michael hopped down from the cab and joined them.

'You look like you've been in an accident, son,' said the officer with the packet, suddenly sounding warm and friendly.

'Why do you say that?' asked Michael.

The officer, a bit taken aback by the boy's cool, defiant, mature manner of speaking, replied, 'Those uniforms issued with no sleeves?'

'I have other tunics which do have sleeves. This particular one does not.'

'You have some identification?'

Prepared and waiting for the question, Michael

presented the cop with his school ID card. The officer considered it.

'Cadet Michael Cutler?'

The officer with the mustache eyed the boy. Then he glanced over at Linc. With a nod of his head toward Linc, he said, 'This man claims to be your father.'

'So he's informed me,' replied Michael.

'How was that again?' asked the officer.

'I said he has informed me of our relationship,' explained the boy.

The officer rubbed a finger across the bristle of his mustache and turned his eyes down to convey to the boy that he had had about enough of his testy answers.

'Well, then, *Mr.* Cutler, why is it that your name's Michael Cutler and his name is Lincoln Hawks? If you're father and son, why don't your last names agree?'

'My grandfather had my name changed legally. I was — it was when I was still a child — known as Michael Hawks. I am now legally known as Michael Cutler.'

'Yeah, why was that? Why'd he change it?'

'Officer,' said Linc in an effort to explain. But the officer held up his hand, indicating he didn't want to hear him. 'Let the boy answer,' he said.

'When I'm twenty-one, I am taking over certain operations within my grandfather's conglomerate. We will then become known as Cutler and Cutler Industries rather than simply Cutler Industries.'

The perplexed officer fumbled with the papers in his hands and tried to get his brain in gear. He stuttered, 'Then this man is not taking you against your will?'

'Officer, are you trying to say I'm being kidnapped? Because if you are, I assure you you've been misinformed. Now, may I please have my ID card back, sir?' said Michael huffily.

The officer handed the card back to the boy. 'Yes, sir,

Mister Cutler,' he said mockingly. He motioned with his head toward the officer holding the dog on the leash.

The officer and the dog headed for the truck and trailer. The dog sniffed. The officer searched. Both were looking for the same thing. Two of the other officers opened the trailer. The two remaining officers stared bullets at Linc. His uneasiness was obvious. He ground his teeth and tried to remain calm.

'Hope your dog likes the smell of onions. That's all he'll pick up on this rig,' said Linc with a smile to the officer wearing the mustache.

The officer cleared a nasal passage and said, 'Yeah? We had a tip to the contrary.'

Linc turned and watched the dog sniffing at the wheels of the truck. The officer watched too. Neither of them noticed Michael walk away and climb back into the cab.

He stood quietly watching the two officers searching inside the truck. As one of the men, a husky pink-faced kid wearing rose-tinted glasses, searched along the wall and near the bunk where the boy had slept the night before, Michael saw him reach inside his jacket. The boy eased himself back where he would not be seen and watched as the officer pulled a plastic bag of white powder from inside his coat. He slipped the bag under the pillow on the bunk. He looked around the room to make sure he had not been seen. Michael remained silent, ducking down out of sight.

Outside the rig, Linc continued to impatiently shift his feet and wait. He looked up at the sound of the German shepherd leading the officer around the truck.

'Nothing under the rig,' said the officer with the dog.

Behind him the officer who had checked inside the trailer climbed down from the rig. 'Trailer's empty. It's clean.'

'Yeah, the cab's clean,' said the officer wearing the

rose-tinted glasses.

The fourth officer standing beside Linc rubbed his cheek with the flat of his hand. 'Well,' said the officer, pulling his hand away from his cheek, 'let's make sure. Eddie, get the dog into the cab. Give him a shot at it.'

On the far side of the cab, Michael eased himself down from the cab and quietly returned to his father's side. Linc reached out and patted the boy on the shoulder, as if to reasure him that everything would be all right.

They watched as the officer with the dog boosted the animal up into the cab. Linc, Michael, and the officers waited uneasily in silence. Then they heard a whoop from inside the rig. Everyone's heads whipped around to see the officer holding the dog with one hand a plastic bag above his head with the other.

'Bingo,' he yelled and hurried the dog down and climbed down behind him.

Linc's eyes narrowed. The gloating officer walked toward him shaking the plastic bag.

'Stashed right under his pillow,' said the officer. 'How the hell did you miss it?' he asked the officer who had planted the bag.

'Damned if I know,' said the husky kid, feigning embarrassment.

'All right, Hawks,' said the officer with the mustache. 'Up against the truck, feet apart, hands up there high — spread 'em wide.'

Linc glared at the man. 'You can't do this,' screamed Linc. Reacting to Linc's rage and the possibility of a hostile prisoner, the officer pulled his revolver and leveled it at Linc's chest.

Spitting the words out with authority, the officer holding the gun said, 'You have the right to remain silent. You have the right to —'

'Stop it!' demanded Michael, yelling above the voice.

The boy shook with fury. His face was red and the muscles stood out on his neck. Like a crusading evangelist, Michael was shaking with righteous indignation, but Linc and the cops had no idea why. Then the boy started to spit out his accusations.

'I saw it!' he said to the officer with the gun. 'I saw him,' he said, pointing his finger at the husky officer wearing the glasses. 'I saw him take the drugs out of his jacket and put them under the pillow.'

The officer holding the gun cut his eyes over at Michael and said, 'Yeah? Well, try to prove that when your old man faces the judge.'

'*His* prints aren't on that bag,' said the boy, collecting himself. He stood squarely, just as he had on meeting Linc in the office. Looking directly into the eyes of the man holding the gun, he said, 'But your officer's prints *are*. But forgetting all that — since I'm sure you have ways to cover them up — I think you'd better know that the governor of this state is one of my grandfather's closest friends. My grandfather contributed more than half of million dollars to his last campaign. Cutler Industries owns four factories in this state employing twenty-six thousand people. Now, either you take that ridiculous bag of dope back where you got it, or I'm getting on the CB and calling every trucker in the area to come in here and be witnesses. And then I shall speak directly to the governor and see that criminal charges are brought against each of you for drug trafficking — as well as a personal civil suit against each of you for trying to harass and damage this man.'

The officers looked at each other. They had egg on their faces and no idea how to get it off. Linc glowed like a proud father. His heart swelled with admiration for his son.

Suddenly the officer holstered his revolver and, without saying a word, wheeled and headed for the car. His fellow officers jerked their heads toward him and decided to follow his example. They shuffled off after him, mum as eggplants.

Linc put his arm on Michael's shoulder, and they stood side by side together and watched the squad cars roar off down the highway. Linc shook his head in awe and said, 'Mike, what can I say?'

'Nothing, sir,' said the boy. 'You saved my life last night. Now we're even.' He lifted his arm and checked the time on his wristwatch. 'But we're running late,' he added. Then he turned and walked away.

Linc shrugged a smile. But he was more than happy. Inside he was shining like the sun.

officer. Khildene made round I found dashed to
follow the example. They shuffled out of him, mumb-
ling arms.

Like put his arm on Earth's shoulders, and they stood
side by side together, and watched the liner taxi out of
down to ... Line shook his head in awe and said
'Blike,' is all each say.

'Nothing,' we said the how. 'You saved my...' He's
might speak, even. He liked his mouth. Further the
jumbo in his waistcoat, but we're empty here, he called
either he turned and walked away.

ph. Line himself's a smile. But he was nodding, but try-
njust he was shining like the sand.

CHAPTER SIX

Jason Cutler leaned back in the high-back leather desk chair. He was listening intently to the message on the phone. He seemed almost bemused by what he was hearing. He closed his eyes and massaged his eyelids with his fingers.

'Michael said all that?' he asked. He was impressed. A Slight smile cracked at the corners of his mouth.

'Umm . . .' he said, considering the information. 'Well, naturally the officers had to back off under those circumstances. They had no way of knowing I was on their side.' He paused and rocked his chair forward and leaned on the panel of the electronic monitor in front of him.

'How do you like that? My own power turned around and used against me. Thank you anyway, Jed.'

He shifted his weight in the chair. He leaned back and crossed his leg over his knee.

'No, you stay out of it from here on. They'll be leaving Tennessee in an hour or so. I'll make other arrangements for the son of a bitch. He'll be in Arkansas soon. I'll be ready for him.'

Cutler hung up the phone and leaned back in his chair. He sat for a moment in thoughtful silence. Then he rocked the chair forward and picked up the phone.

As Linc's rig crossed the bridge over the Mississippi, Linc turned to Michael and said, 'We're in Arkansas now.'

'I can read, sir,' said the boy.

'Yeah,' said Linc. 'You'd think a smart boy like you could see things clearly. But I don't think you do.'

'I see some things clearly,' said Michael. He paused and looked over at his father and added, 'Sometimes a little too clearly to be happy.'

'That's an important word, Mike. The key word — happy.' He nodded his head at the boy and gave him the wink of experience. 'What you said back there to Smoky — about going into business with your grandfather when you turn twenty-one — you really want to do that?'

'That's what I'm trained for.'

'I got something better than that in mind for you,' said his father, 'and you don't have to wait 'til you're twenty-one.'

'Forget it, sir.'

'Forget it? I haven't even told you what it is.'

'I already know.'

'Yeah,' said Linc doubtfully. 'So what is it?'

'You expect my mother to leave the ranch,' said Michael with a bored sigh, 'take me out of school, and come and live with you.'

'Son of a bitch!' said Linc with surprise. 'Did *I* say that?' he asked, laying his hand across his chest and giving the boy an open-mouthed, 'Who me?' expression.

'You said you're going to parlay this truck and first prize in some Las Vegas arm-wrestling contest into a trucking company. You said you came back to get your family together. What other conclusion *could* I make?' asked the boy very logically.

'Well, I didn't tell you about your part in the business.'

'Me in a trucking business? I'm not looking forward to spending my life with grease on my hands.'

Linc glanced over at the boy and thought for a moment, considering the kid's cut-down job on him.

'You don't think that I'm as smart as your grandpa, do you?' Linc asked.

'Not even remotely, sir,' said the boy, not bothering to look at his father.

'That dumb, huh?' asked Linc calmly.

'I didn't say you were dumb,' said the boy, trying to save Linc's feelings. 'You simply never had an opportunity to get the kind of education I'm getting. That's why you ended up getting a Spec 4 in Nam, not an officer. That's why you did manual labor in the merchant marines and drive a truck — and arm-wrestle.'

Linc cocked his head and shrugged, as if mocking Michael's upper crust attitude toward him.

'I guess that tells me where I stand on the social scale.'

Michael continued. It was as if he was tutoring his father and it was hard, boring work, but Linc Hawks might as well know the facts, so he continued, 'The average mental age of an adult is fourteen — just two years older than I am.' He paused and looked at his father. Linc did not take his eyes off the road. The boy decided to level with the old man. 'For truckers it has to be somewhere in the ten- to twelve-year-old range.'

'That you speaking,' asked Linc, 'or Grandpa?'

Michael curled his lip and shook his head. Linc began to slow the truck. Very gently, he eased the big baby over onto the shoulder of the road and brought the rig to a stop. He killed the power. For a moment the two sat in silence.

Michael said nothing. He expected his father to lambaste his for his slam on the truckers. But Linc did not speak.

'Why have we stopped, sir?'

Linc erupted with fury. 'Because I goddamn resent what you said about truckers. Some of the smartest men I know drive long-haul rigs across this country. It takes brains and know-how and guts to push one of these monsters night

99

and day from coast to coast, with all the regulations and accounting records and weigh-ins and asshole cops breathing down your neck. Now, you're such a little genius you just slip over here into *my* seat and you see if *you* can drive this sucker.'

Before Michael could even reply, Linc had thrown open the door and climbed down from the cab. He slammed the door behind him and started for the other side of the truck.

For a moment Michael sat, his arms folded, stoic and unmoved. He watched his father walking in front of the truck, heading for the other side. Defiantly, he bumped himself over into the driver's seat.

Linc jerked the passenger door open and eyed the boy sitting under the wheel. 'She's all yours, Einstein.'

Michael rolled his eyes over in the direction of his father. Linc opened his hands to the highway. Michael looked down at the dashboard. It might as well have been the panel on a 747. Gauges surrounded by buttons, switches, and levers seemed to confront him on all sides. He had no idea where to begin, and he didn't dare ask.

Meanwhile, Linc made the most of the situation. He slipped his boots off and propped his feet up on the padded dash. He leaned himself back and rested his hands behind his head. 'C'mon, boy, we got some miles to make.'

Frustrated but unwilling to admit defeat, Michael complained, 'This is an unfair test — like my putting you in front of a PC and asking you to program a spread sheet. Everybody needs instruction. I've never driven a truck.'

'So?'

'So you have to check me out.'

'Why ask me?' said Linc condescendingly. 'I'm only a dumb trucker. You're the one with all the brains.'

Seeing that his father was as strong-willed and stubborn as he was, the boy realized he was going to get nowhere

100

with him. So he decided to go for it on his own. He flipped the key in the switch. Nothing happened. Linc closed his eyes and half smiled. Michael decided to take a chance and hit one of the buttons that looked as if it might be a starter button. With the push of the button, the semi's long-range driving lights kicked on. Michael quickly jabbed them off and took a go at another switch. The air conditioner sprang to life, moaning and blowing. Michael exhaled and shot a hateful glance over at his father.

Linc squinted one eye open and said, 'Don't quit now. You got a load of auxiliaries you haven't even begun to find.'

The father's sarcasm made the boy more determined to get the engine running. He haphazardly flicked one switch after another, each producing mayhem rather than a humming motor.

'Not a fair test,' screeched the boy.

'I don't know why you're having such a hard time. Nothing to it,' said Linc, lording it over the kid. He reached across the boy's body and flicked on the power. In a second the glow-plug lights indicated that the diesel could be started.

Linc opened his hands to the boy to show him that there was nothing to it. Michael tried his best to ignore his hotdogging father. But he listened carefully when Linc said, 'Don't touch the accelerator yet.'

Linc pointed to a silver button on the dash. Michael looked down at it. He pressed it. At last the big diesel started to churn. It was music to Michael's ears. At that moment it was better than Talking Heads and B-52s combined. As he felt the power building under his control, Michael started to smile. It felt good. It made him feel powerful.

'Okay, junior jammer, she's all yours.'

Michael tentatively eased his foot onto the accelerator

and looked into the side mirror. Then, believe it or not, the uneasy, nervous little boy waddled the big tractor-trailer onto the highway. With gears grinding and the rig lurching and sliding along, the Silver Hawk headed for Little Rock.

Inside the cab Linc continued to play the role of unconcerned bystander. He waited for the boy to show him how easy it was to be a truck driver. Nevertheless, he carefully monitored every move the boy was attempting to make. When the gears started to do the kid in, Linc reached across and guided the boy's hand into an upper gear.

'Easy, gear bonger, you gotta have the clutch in *all* the way. You're not ready to float gears yet.'

The boy was too nervous to take his eyes from the road, even though the highway seemed deserted. He had not seen a car, but just steering the big clipper ship was making him swallow his heart every time his stomach brought it up. But as the truck gained speed, the kid grew with confidence. Even his sidewinder pattern on the highway was beginning to straighten out.

The performance pleased Linc. He observed the boy's death-lock grip on the steering wheel. But still the rig wandered, and Linc warned him, 'Try bringing it back over to our side of the road. Those double lines in the center may make it easy to aim, but it plays hell with your safety factor.'

Michael stiffly and apprehensively turned the wheel to the right. The truck did the same. The boy smiled with his success.

'Now, that didn't hurt much did it?' asked Linc.

'What didn't, sir?' said the boy, still too nervous to talk and drive at the same time.

'Smiling,' said Linc, smiling himself.

The boy did not look at Linc. He was too scared to look away from the road, but he kept smiling, and so did Linc.

'It's really exhilarating, isn't it? Almost as good as riding a horse,' said Michael with real pleasure in his voice.

Linc thought the remark was a little strange, so he asked, 'You ride?'

'Frankly, sir, it's the only thing I can do well. You saw my swimming. But my riding is really okay,' he said. Then, in an effort to explain it fully, he added, 'I mean, after all, growing up on a ranch — if you can't ride you might as well be dead.'

Lincoln was pleased to hear his son was a good rider. And it gave him the beginnings of an idea.

As Linc and Michael came strolling out of an Arkansas diner, Linc danced away from his son, hiding something behind his back. He backed away from the boy, grinning, wanting Mike to try and see the surprise. But the boy refused to go for the bait.

'Which hand?' teased Linc.

'I don't eat potato chips, sir.'

'It's not potato chips, dammit! Which hand?' But the boy only shook his head and kept walking.

'It's a present,' exhorted Linc. 'A surprise.'

Unenthused, Michael said, 'Left hand,' just to placate his father.

His father smiled and brought up his left hand. Between his fingers he held a cassette tape. With a bow at the waist, Linc presented the tape to Michael. The boy took the tape and with one quick glance he exclaimed, 'Talking Heads! It's the new album — in Arkansas? I haven't been able to get it in Virginia.'

Obviously pleased by his son's reaction, Linc said, 'Well, now you see how all of us dumb truckers stick together. Last time you dozed off in the cab, I got on the CB and bounced a message all the way up to Tulsa. Got a buddy of mine who's coming this way to pick up the tape and meet me here. The guy I introduced you to in the diner — Alex.'

The boy nodded that he remembered him. 'He brought it to me. Straight from Tulsa,' said Linc.

'Thank you, sir,' said the boy, truly pleased and more than a little impressed. 'I'll make a deal with you — for every time I play this between here and Dallas, you may play Kenny Rogers.'

Linc grinned and said, 'Hey, now that's very decent of you — considering that it's my stereo.'

Michael shrugged sheepishly. Linc laughed and extended an open palm. The boy slapped the hand. Linc grabbed the boy by the shoulders and gave him a happy dad slap on the bottom. They walked to the gas pumps together. There was a lightness in their footsteps.

As they neared the rig, the gas station attendant, a skinny school kid named Tommy, said, 'She took a hundred sixty gallons of diesel and two quarts of oil. Wanna run it up, Linc?'

Linc did a double take at the question. 'That'd be like betting against myself, Tommy. Hoping to win in Vegas next weekend. If I do, I won't be coming through here for a long, long time. Put it on the long green.'

'Comes to eighty-five oh four. Hope you win, Linc,' said the attendant, 'but we'll sure miss you.'

'Thanks,' said Linc, fishing cash out of his jeans in stages until he had piled ninety dollars in the boy's hand. The boy went inside the cash booth, rang up the purchase, and pulled Linc's change from the register. He returned and counted the change into Linc's hand. Linc squeezed the bills around the coins and shoved the money into his jeans.

Linc said, 'Next time you see me I'll be on my way to leading my own fleet.' He winked at the boy.

*

The Talking Heads were talking, but Linc wasn't listening. He paid no attention to the music. It wasn't the music that interested him. Michael's reaction to the new tape meant much more to him. The tape had transformed the uptight, stiff-backed little monster he'd picked up at the school into something Linc believed to be more like the average twelve-year-old. Michael sat with his eyes closed, grooving with the beat. Linc enjoyed watching the boy's relaxed state for a few moments, then turned his eyes back to the highway.

Down the road in the middle of the highway he saw a semi blocking the highway. Linc could see a group of men with flashlights flagging him down. Linc slowed the rig and approached the men very slowly. Michael opened his eyes and asked, 'What is it?'

'I dunno,' said Linc.

As one of the men, a young man in a blue-jean jacket and western hat, approached the cab, Linc brought the window down.

The young man called out, 'Hey, buddy, you got anything in your first-aid for cardiac arrest?'

'Somebody have a heart attack?' asked Linc.

'Yeah, looks like it.'

Linc opened the door and started to climb down from the cab. Suddenly the man lunged for Linc and pulled him to the ground. Immediately, the other men were on him. Michael threw himself at the door to try and aid his father, but he was instead greeted by two men. One of them, a bushy-bearded man, pulled the boy from the cab and dragged him screaming toward a blue Chevy pickup with Texas plates.

In the glare of the rig's headlights, Michael saw his father spin free from the cowboy and send the jean-jacketed man to the ground with a backhanded smash across the throat. As the three other men tried to close in and overpower him, Linc became a whirling dervish of flailing elbows and knees, making it almost impossible for the men to land a halfway punishing punch.

What the men did not realize was that Lincoln Hawks was no ordinary fighter. Linc was more than just an experienced street brawler. He had learned his fighting skills brawling in the alleys of Asia. He knew Thai boxing. His elbows and knees were lethal weapons.

Stunned by the elbow smashes to their heads, two of the men fell back, groggy and confused. Spinning to face the fourth man, the only one of the four still standing, Linc delivered a tremendous two-handed palm clap to the man's eardrums. The man went deaf, but Linc was not finished. Still holding the head with one hand, Linc drove an elbow into his jaw. Then, grabbing the man's head, he pulled it down to meet the knee he had coming up. The man's head cracked, and he fell face forward onto the highway.

As he delivered the knee smash, Linc pivoted like a center delivering a sky hook. He stood facing the two remaining men.

Behind him the cowboy was on his knees wheezing and coughing, trying to breathe and bring up the blood clogged in his throat.

The other man lay motionless on the highway.

As one of the men, a rotund, balding rock, charged Linc, his partner, a taller man with long blond hair hanging out from under a baseball cap, made the stupid mistake of trying to take Linc from behind by grabbing him in a neck lock.

Linc grabbed the arm in his powerful hands and brought the dumb bastard's arm down with such force over his own shoulder that the elbow disconnected. Not content to abandon the man screaming in pain, Linc slammed him to the asphalt and stomped down on the sternum.

Trying to take advantage of Linc's dedication to destruction, the fat boy connected with a right cross to Linc's jaw. But as he took the punch, he palm-heeled baldy's elbow and spun the man around. As they exchanged blows, Linc took two for one gladly, never flinching or showing any signs of pain or damage. Once he had his hands on the fat man, Linc torqued his body three times, each time burying his knee up into the man's kidneys and rib cage. When Linc released the man, he dropped to his knees, spitting blood.

Meanwhile, the two hulks had found that dealing with Michael was not an easy task either. The boy twisted and bit and spat and kicked and screamed. He could not escape, but he was making it difficult for them to load him into the truck.

With all four of Linc's punks moaning on the ground, he charged Michael's abductors. He grabbed the red-bearded man by the hair and yanked him so violently it was almost a bare-handed scalping. But the man's head followed the yank and turned to meet the explosive smash of Linc's elbow in his face. Linc followed the blow with a series of swift blows to the redhead's face and neck. When Linc finally released the man's hair, the man's beard was stained with blood. The man fell against the pickup and slid down the fender to the ground. Realizing that he was now alone against this crazy truck driver, the man holding Michael threw the boy aside and flipped the glove compartment open of the pickup. But before the man could grasp what he was reaching for, Linc slammed the lid of the compartment shut on the man's wrist. The force of the metal ripped into the man's arm, severing his artery. Blood sprayed a fine mist across the windshield. The man screamed in agony, but Linc ignored the man's cries. He spun the man around, drove combinations into the man's chest and sternum. The man staggered and stumbled forward, holding his bleeding arm.

Still fueled with rage and anger, Linc tore into the glove compartment and pulled out the .44 magnum the man had been trying to find.

With the gun held tightly in both his hands police-officer style, Linc moved in front of the pickup and leveled the magnum on the radiator. The powerful handgun kicked twice. Hissing steam belched from under the hood. Then he trotted away to the truck blocking the road and put four shots into the engine block.

Satisfied, he heaved the pistol into the darkness and ran back to Michael.

'You okay?' asked Linc, panting and gasping for breath. The boy nodded.

'You sure?'

'I'm okay,' said Michael, catching his breath.

Finally Linc began to calm down. He said, 'I had my eye on you all the time. You did great.'

The boy said nothing. Linc dropped his arm around him. The boy's uniform jacket was torn almost off him. His T-shirt was stretched and ripped. Linc tugged at the torn clothes, trying to reshape him. They walked to the truck arm in arm.

'This is the second attack,' said the boy. 'Why?'

'Third,' said Linc. 'Don't forget those cops.'

Michael shook his head in confusion. 'I can't understand why my grandfather would go to such extremes simply to keep us apart.' He looked at Linc. Linc did not rush in to answer. He continued walking, saying nothing. 'He's one of the richest men in the world. Why would he hire men like this?'

'Because he's an alley fighter — just like me,' said Linc. 'He figures you fight fire with fire.'

As they walked past the battered, bleeding cowboy, Michael grimaced. He looked up at his father and asked, 'Shouldn't we call an ambulance or something?'

'I guess that would be the Christian thing to do,' said Linc.

The boy looked at his father with misgivings. Linc shrugged it off. 'They'll live. If I'd wanted to kill them, I could have. But why should I let them off easy?'

It was night when they left Arkansas and crossed into Oklahoma. Kenny Rogers was playing on the tape deck.

Linc said, 'I bet you don't know that not too far from here — at Fort Sill — a little more then a hundred years ago the last of the Comanches rode in and gave up their weapons.'

'I bet *you* wouldn't have. You'd have died first,' said the boy.

A slight grin creased Linc's face. The boy's response surprised him, but he liked it. 'I'll take that as a compliment, but I don't know what I would have done. The chief leading them was a half-breed.'

Michael turned and looked at him. This time the look in the boy's eyes was less hostile. He seemed for the first time almost curious.

'His name was Quanah Parker. His mother was a white woman. He fought to the very end. He was the last Comanche leader to surrender. He kept fighting when the others were signing peace treaties. He never signed anything. You know what he told them?'

The boy shook his head.

'He said, "Let the bluecoats come and whip me." They never did. He was a pretty salty dude. I appreciate the compliment, but to think that I would have outlasted Quanah Parker is going some. I think he probably did the right thing — for his people. If it'd just been him, maybe he'd have done something else. Sometimes you do things you don't want to. But you do it for the good of somebody else. Even when they don't know it's for them. . . .'

He paused. His words trailed off. He stared down the highway. His eyes seemed far away. The boy looked at him almost compassionately and said, 'I've been hard on you, haven't I?'

'Yeah, you sure have. But I gotta tell you, Mike, even though you were drawing blood, I was proud of you. You're a kid that doesn't take crap from anybody. I may want to get my hands on your grandfather, but I have to admit the bastard's done *something* right. He's made you a survivor. All the rest of his shit ain't worth talking about — it's just shit.'

Michael listened carefully, but he didn't respond. He just listened.

'Hangin' in — that's what life is, Mike. That's what arm wrestling is. Nothing else.'

Michael wanted to speak, but the words wouldn't come. Finally he forced them. His voice quivered. 'I can't tell you how many times I cried — wondering why you left — wondering what I'd done to make you leave.' His voice broke. Tears started to trickle from his eyes.

'That's over. Behind us. We both know why I'm back. Because I love you,' said Linc.

Michael said nothing. He sniffed and tried to hold back the tears, but he couldn't. Linc flashed him a look of understanding — as if to say, it's all right, go ahead and cry. There was nothing more for either of them to say.

They drove for miles without speaking. Kenny Rogers continued to serenade them, but neither of them heard the music. It was simply background noise, playing under their thoughts — thoughts of other times, other places.

Linc pulled the truck off the highway and onto a country road that cut into the Kiamichi Mountains. As the big rig wound its way through the rugged mountain countryside, Michael began to wonder why they had left the main highway for this deserted, winding road, but he didn't question his father this time. He figured he would learn soon enough. But when the headlights flashed across a sign that read 'Comanche Indian Reservation,' he decided he'd waited long enough for an explanation.

He asked, 'Why are we turning off here?'

'I want you to see something.'

They rolled on through the reservation ground. When they had gone four or five miles, Linc stopped the rig and threw his door open. 'C'mon,' he said.

They got out of the rig and walked across an open pasture. Linc said, 'Wait here. Don't move.' Then he walked away. In front of him Michael sensed movement, but even under the stars he could not tell what it was. Then lights flashed. Before him, bathed in the glare of floodlights, stood twelve Arabian horses stirring inside a corral.

Stunned by the sight, Michael moved like a zombie toward the wooden fence. He climbed to the top rung of the fence and rested himself. Linc hurried to him and climbed up beside him.

'What d'ya think of 'em?' asked Linc.

'They're beautiful What kind are they?'

'Arabians.'

'Arabians?' asked Micheal with surprise.

'That's right. The finest horses in the world — about the smartest horses there are.'

Michael was impressed. He knew horses. He valued them. But before he could comment on Linc's idea, a man's voice cried out from somewhere in the darkness, 'Linc!'

They turned and saw a man sliding out of the shadows. The boy could not see the man clearly, but he could see he was big. He was huge. In the man's hand was a rifle.

For an instant Michael believed it was the arrival of more trouble, but when Linc turned and ran to the man, the boy relaxed. He walked over to where the two men stood embracing one another.

Linc separated from the man and turned toward the boy.

'Michael,' said Linc, raising his voice happily, 'I want you to meet my friend White Wolf. I call him Ap — "Father," in our language.'

Michael's eyes ran up the looming hulk that dwarfed him. The boy was awed by the giant. The man was like a tall pine, perfectly straight and symmetrical. He wore his raven hair parted in the middle of his forehead all the way back to the crown, forming a braid on each side. Down the center of the part was a streak of red paint. The long black braids were tied with bright red cloth. In the helix of one ear he wore six circles of brass. No one had to tell the boy that the man was Comanche. And no one had to remind him of his manners. He said, 'Good evening, sir.'

'This is Michael,' said Linc, 'my one and only son.'

White Wolf stared down at the boy, not speaking, just looking the boy over. Then he asked, 'Do you like horses?'

'Very much, sir.'

'Here,' said White Wolf, handing the boy a headband. The boy glanced at his father. Linc's eyes indicated he should take it.

'Yours,' said White Wolf as the boy took the gift. 'When we ride, wear it.'

'Are we planning to ride?' asked the boy.

'We're spending the rest of the weekend here,' said Linc. 'First thing Monday morning we'll drive straight to Dallas. You can pick any horse you want.'

They rode into the moonlit mountains and followed the trails made many years before. They rode the canyons.

Birds fluttered and flew away. Small animals ran for cover at the sound of the galloping horses. They rode together and looked remarkably like three Indians.

The three horses moved almost in unison, their proud heads lined up.

But as they rode, each rider saw a different movie in his mind. White Wolf rode with the memories of a small boy riding with him. The young boy was Linc, and it was White Wolf teaching the young Comanche boy to ride. His movie was from the past. Memories filled his head.

For Linc, he rode with flashing quick cuts of himself and Christina riding together. They were young, smiling, and happy. They were in love. His movie was a love story; the glory days with Christina.

The boy's movie was not based on memories. He relied on imagination. He saw himself in a past he'd never known, a past he would never know except in his mind — riding the mountains in the moonlight. He saw himself as a Comanche boy riding to save his people. He did not dream of memories of precious moments or true love. He dreamed of being a hero.

As they rode back to the truck, the boy hollered a loud war whoop, and leaning low on his mount, he broke away and thundered down the hill to the corral.

Linc and White Wolf raced their horses to the corral. They hit the gate neck and neck. At the finish the two men jumped from their horses and embraced one another.

Michael sat at the edge of the gate with his bridle and reins dangling from his hands. He watched the two men laughing and joking as they slipped the bridles off their mounts.

The boy had never seen this kind of open, boisterous affection between two people before. It was a new experience for him. But he liked it. Just watching them made him feel good inside.

'You're a pretty good rider,' said Linc, walking over to the boy.

'Thanks,' said Michael, obviously pleased by his father's compliment.

'Are you hungry?'

'Yes, sir.'

'Good,' said White Wolf. 'I had a big catch today. Mountain trout.'

'That qualifies as health food, doesn't it?' teased Linc.

'Yes, sir,' said Michael. 'Trout are an excellent food source.'

White Wolf did something of a double take at the comment. He cut his eyes over at Linc, who said, 'Private joke.' White Wolf nodded and said, 'Let's head for the house then. I'm hungry as a bear.'

White Wolf's house was a combination of logs and mortar with a frame section that had apparently been added to enlarge the space. Unlike some of the unfortunate reservation Indians and Oklahoma farmers, White Wolf in his own modest way had avoided the hard times that had hit many of his friends.

He was a proud man who was good with horses, a smart trader, and a good hunter and fisherman. He had used all three skills to better himself and become financially safe and independent of the white man's world of pressures and headaches.

White Wolf prepared the mountain trout with beans and hash brown potatoes and biscuits. Michael ate heartily. He asked no questions and made no complaints.

As they ate, White Wolf told Michael about the Comanches. 'The word Comanche means enemy, or more accurately, it means anyone who wants to fight me.' Linc raised his eyebrows at Michael. The boy acknowledged Linc's facial gesture with a half grin but remained absorbed in White Wolf's narration.

'In sign language we were known always as the Snakes. There are stories about where the name came from. One of them tells how when a wolf howled in front of a band of Comanches traveling south, some of the group considered it a warning. They turned back. Those that remained picked a new chief and went south. After that those that moved on called those that went back snakes. Pretty soon the name stuck for all Comanches.

'The Comanches lived on buffalo meat — our band was the Buffalo Eaters. They got the name because they always had plenty buffalo to eat. We were always moving, so finding the buffalo was important. The other thing that was important was the horse. Comanches are great horsemen. That's why you ride so well — your Comanche blood.'

Michael cut his eyes over to his father. Linc rolled his eyes to the ceiling and pretended to be silently whistling.

'But most of all,' continued White Wolf, 'Comanches were warriors. In the same way you are learning the way of the modern-day warrior, Michael, Comanche boys learned very early too the way of the warrior. He was trained. Just like you are being trained.'

'Was my father trained as a warrior?' asked Michael.

'Yes, he was.'

Linc nodded his head. 'Oh, yes,' said Linc. 'I had quite a teacher.'

'When your father was a boy he came to me to learn the Indian ways. I saw the reflection of the Comanche spirit in him. Though my people told me the white man could never learn our ways, I decided to instruct him. I knew he would make me proud. I have never regreted my decision.'

Linc leaned back in his chair and opened his hands outward and pleaded to Michael, 'Now you know why I turned out the way I did. It's all *his* fault.'

115

White Wolf cut his penetrating dark eyes over to Linc and continued his story.

'One of the ways we used to keep children in line was to tell them stories about the Big Cannibal Owl who lived in a nearby cave and came out at night to eat bad children. It didn't work with your father. He took his bow and arrows and went out to hunt the Cannibal Owl.'

Linc winked at the boy and said, 'Got him too. We ate him for Thanksgiving dinner.'

Michael seemed mesmerized by White Wolf's stories. A whole new world of knowledge had suddenly opened to him, and being an intelligent, inquisitive twelve-year-old with a rich imagination, his mind was alive with questions.

The wide-eyed youngster asked the Comanche story-teller about his father. 'Where did he get the name Silver Hawk?'

White Wolf rubbed his forehead with his fingertips and answered.

'When he was six he held a hawk's wing in each hand and tried to fly off the top of a tree.'

The puzzled Michael said, 'Yes . . . but hawks are black. Why *Silver* Hawk?'

'To you, hawks are black. But to other hawks — they're silver.'

Michael pondered the answer for a moment, trying to determine how White Wolf would know what color a hawk was to other hawks. He wanted to ask the question, but he felt it would be disrespectful. He wondered how hawks knew color anyway. He was going to ask about that when White Wolf shoved the dirty dinner dishes across the table toward him. Michael did not understand what was happening. But when White Wolf raised his massive arm and placed his elbow on the table and opened his hand, the boy realized he was in for another round of arm wrestling. The boy glanced at his father. He saw Linc brace himself

116

and raise his arm to the table. The warriors were going to test themselves. The teacher had challenged the student.

'Whenever you're ready,' said White Wolf.

Linc locked his fingers around the huge hand of his uncle and positioned himself. 'Ready,' said Linc. 'Go!'

The two arms jerked, resisting the force being leveled against them. Michael watched as his father strained against White Wolf's long, muscular arm. But slowly, not suddenly and decisively as in his victory over the Smasher, Linc began to force his uncle's arm down. The veins in White Wolf's arm swelled to the size of pencils. His face flushed with blood as he tried to resist the relentless pressure against his upper-body strength. But the arm continued to go down . . . down . . . and then . . . *touch.*

Linc exploded with a lung full of air. He shook his head and rose from his seat, dangling his arm. He opened and closed his hand, trying to get feeling into it again.

'Now I *know* I'm ready!' he said to Michael. He continued to dance about the table, rubbing the circulation back into his arm. White Wolf remained seated, silent and stoic. He rotated his arm, like a baseball pitcher loosening a stiff shoulder.

'I never took him before, not in my whole life,' exclaimed the jubilant Linc. 'It's because you were here, Mike,' he added, slapping the boy on the shoulder happily. 'I *had* to take him.'

White Wolf rose from his seat and walked to the doorway of the kitchen. He paused and looked back at the two of them. Very softly he said, 'Come.'

In a clearing near White Wolf's ranch house, Linc sat on the ground with his legs folded in front of him. He was naked except for a breechcloth and headband. His muscled body glistened in the light of the campfire burning before him. His face was painted red. His eyelids were white. His cheeks were streaked with black.

Michael stood in the flickering shadows of the fire. He watched White Wolf lay a circle of red paint around the area of Linc and the fire.

When the circle was completed, he began to paint inside the ring. He created beautiful patterns of intricate design in the sand with bright colors.

Once he had laid down the colors, he moved out of the circle using a pattern of widening circular steps, leaving Linc all alone.

White Wolf walked into the darkness and picked up a burlap bag he had placed beside a tree. He was careful to lift the bag by the top, and he carried it held away from him.

Michael stood in the dark, still confused by what was happening. White Wolf walked to the edge of the circle and jerked the string at the mouth of the bag, opening it. With one swift, fluid motion, he shook the contents of the bag into the circle and jumped away.

A large rattlesnake plopped on the ground in front of Linc. Michael gasped at the sight of the snake and broke to run to his father. But White Wolf held out an arm and restrained him. The boy's apprehensive eyes rolled up and appealed to White Wolf for help. But the big Commanche did not speak. His firm grip on the boy's shoulder and the stern look on the man's face indicated that other forces were now at work — forces that he had never experienced, laws and rules and a way of life that he did not know or even understand. So the boy relaxed and stepped back and trained his eyes on the rattlesnake. The snake slithered about on the ground and coiled and raised its angry head.

Almost instantly it focused on Linc's painted face. Immediately, the snake signaled war with a dry rattling shake of the tail.

Michael knew he could not help his father. He knew

White Wolf would stop him. It was clear that he was not supposed to interfere, but he wanted to cry out. He wanted to yell a warning to his father. His brain was sending signals to his tongue to speak. He could feel the words forming in his throat, but the sounds did not come. The overpowering, massive presence of White Wolf smothered any action that might spoil the moment.

Linc remained perfectly still. His eyes were half closed. He seemed to be in a trance, only partly aware of the events occurring around him.

But Michael remembered Linc's zombie-like trance at Martha's truck stop. He had prepared for his match there by going into some sort of strange, otherworldly hocus-pocus. It was obvious to Michael that it was happening again. The warrior was preparing for war — war with a snake?

Michael saw his father's eyes open. They opened slowly, just as they had done at the diner. The rattlesnake moved closer, raising its head to be in position to strike.

Linc lowered his head in the direction of the snake. Easing his head down to the snake's level, Linc held his head only inches from the reptile's eyes. He seemed to be tempting — even inviting — the snake to strike.

Frozen in fear and tense to the bone, Michael watched his father stare at the snake face to face, eye to eye. Each held its ground. Each waited for the other to make a move.

Almost as calm and still was White Wolf. He stood firm and straight, staring without emotion, but not without intensity, at the confrontation in the ring. His hand remained firm on Michael's shoulder, and his gaze rivaled the snake's for concentrated direction.

For what seemed like minutes but in reality was only seconds, Linc and the snake remained in their long stare-down, waiting for the other to blink.

At last the snake seemed to decide that there was a

center of calmness about the stranger. The snake began to lower its head. It had decided the creature was not a threat. Perceiving this, Linc blew into the reptile's face. Immediately, the snake reacted. Angrily it recoiled, ready to strike.

Suddenly, with a swiftness that was imperceptible to the eye, the snake struck. But immediately, Linc's right hand darted out and closed around the snake's neck just below its gaping fangs.

Michael's eyes could not believe what they had seen Linc had grabbed the striking snake before it struck his face. He held the snake in his hand and rose from the ground. He turned his body to face the west. He lifted his eyes to the moon. In his heart was the ancient Death Song of the Kiowa:

> I live, but I shall not live forever.
> Mysterious Moon, you only remain,
> Powerful Sun, you alone remain,
> Wonderful Earth, only you live forever.

He was offering thanks; a prayer was in his heart. He knew that he had teased death and walked away smiling.

He lifted the snake above his head and let the serpent wiggle. For a long moment, like a statue to victory, he stood holding the vanquished warrior above his head.

Then, like the happy warrior he was, he shouted a glorious, triumphant war cry of victory and tossed the wriggling snake to freedom in the bushes. He turned toward White Wolf and Michael. A big, glorious smile spread across his face like a southwestern sunrise.

Michael sagged, completely drained by the ordeal. White Wolf showed no emotion, only approval. He nodded his head and said, '*Now* you are ready.'

120

CHAPTER SEVEN

The Talking Heads blasted from the stereo, but the words of White Wolf still rang in Linc's ears as the rig rolled down the interstate toward Dallas. The skyline of the city rose in the distance.

Linc was pushing the rig hard to complete the second leg of his mission — to visit Christina with his son. In just a few minutes he'd be seeing her again, with the son they both loved. Behind him in the sleeper compartment, Michael lounged on the bunk. He lay on his back with his hands behind his head, staring up at the bulkhead of photographs chronicling the twelve years of his life.

He called out to his father. Over the blast of the Talking Heads, Linc heard, 'Sir?'

'What?' yelled Linc, turning down the roar of the music.

'Did mother really send these pictures to you?'

'Sure. I couldn't very well make them myself.'

The boy rolled over on his side and lay his head on his hand, with his elbow supported on the bed.

'Why didn't she tell me?' he mumbled to himself. 'Why didn't she tell me?'

Linc lifted his head, thinking the question was for him, and said, 'Probably afraid you'd tell your grandpa.'

Michael rolled over and sat up on the side of the bed.

'That's unfair, sir,' said the boy. 'I'd never do anything to hurt my mother.'

'You ever tell her that?'

There was no answer. Linc turned his head back toward the sleeper, then turned his eyes back to the road. The boy's answer came after a long pause.

'No, sir,' was the soft reply.

'Then how would she know?' asked Linc.

Michael buried his head in his hands and stared at the floor. It was a tough question. Michael didn't know the answer. He'd have to think some more, and thinking was a very torturous business when you didn't know the answers.

Linc was scanning the sides of the road for directions when he saw it: a sign that read: DALLAS MEMORIAL HOSPITAL. At the turnoff he guided the truck and trailer into the right-hand lane and exited onto the road leading to the hospital.

At the information window of the hospital, Linc waited patiently. White Wolf and Michael stood to one side. Linc shifted his weight from foot to foot and smiled an understanding smile at Michael.

Ahead of him, a deeply lined farmer from Sulphur Springs held his white Stetson in his hand while talking to the teenage redhead wearing a pink nurse's uniform. The farmer's wife wore a plain green dress and black low-heeled shoes. She held a black purse in her hand.

'I know one thing,' said the farmer. 'If I ever get outta this place, it'll be a cold day in July before I come back.'

The teenager in the information booth smiled.

'This traffic is just too fast for us,' said his wife.

'It's pretty bad,' said the girl. 'Is there anything else you want to know? You think you can find your way now?'

'I doubt it,' said the farmer. 'But like the bobtail cow said about trying to swish flies, "It won't hurt none t' try." '

Linc grinned and waited. The farmer and his wife turned

to leave. He looked up and saw Linc and said, 'Hi, chief.' The wife tugged at her husband's sleeve, and they walked away toward the exit.

Linc stepped up to the window and, smiling, asked, 'Think they'll make it?'

The teenager smiled and shook her head.

'I don't know,' she said. 'They sure were lost. Their preacher was operated on this morning.'

Linc nodded understanding and said, 'Has Mrs. Christina Hawks been assigned her room?'

The young girl turned to her display terminal and read the response to her input. She looked up at Linc and said, 'I'm sorry, sir, but we have no record of a pending room assignment for Mrs. Christina Hawks. Was she expected today?'

Linc leaned on the information window ledge and said, 'About an hour ago. She's scheduled for surgery Wednesday morning.'

Behind the young girl, a clerk busy filling out a clipboard form raised her head.

'Let me try Wednesday,' said the girl. Linc shrugged. But as the girl began her input for Wednesday the woman behind her said, 'Pat.'

The girl turned and saw the older clerk motion her over.

'Excuse me,' she said to Linc. She rose and huddled with the older woman. Linc turned away from the women, toward Michael. He signaled an 'I don't know what's up' gesture to them and turned back to the window.

The women were still talking softly. Both were glancing over at Linc. Suddenly he realized that the whispering was about Christina.

The young girl returned to the window with the older woman. The older clerk, a short, dark-haired, plump woman, held the clipboard against her chest and, looking up at Linc, asked, 'Sir, are you a relative of the patient you asked about?'

With obvious concern, Linc said, 'Yes, I'm her husband.'

The woman blinked. 'Sir,' she said, 'perhaps you'd like to talk to one of our staff doctors.'

'I don't need a staff doctor. Just tell me,' said Linc demandingly.

The woman hesitated, blinked her eyes once more, and, looking straight at Linc, said, 'She died Saturday night.'

'Died?'

'I think you should speak with Dr. Dietrich. We'll send for him.'

'It won't be necessary,' said Linc. He wiped his face with his hand and turned his back to the window. He looked at Michael.

It was the same boy Linc had picked up at military school, but he hardly looked the same. All that was left of his unform was the torn trousers he was wearing. The tunic had been discarded for a T-shirt. On his head he wore the headband given him by White Wolf. But the most dramatic and significant change that Linc saw in the boy was in his face. The boy was smiling.

Linc knew there was no easy way. He wanted to find a way, but he knew there was no way to avoid what was coming. He took a deep breath and let it out. He shoved his fingers into the pockets of his jeans and walked over to Michael.

He knew at first glance that something was wrong. The smile on Michael's face wilted when he saw the concern in his father's eyes.

'What's the matter, sir?'

Linc looked at the boy. He took a breath and reached out for the boy, to try and comfort him, to hold him, to give him something to lean on. But the boy backed away. His eyes glared with distrust. 'What is it? What's wrong?'

'We're too late. She . . .' He hesitated. 'Your mother's

dead, Michael.' Before Linc could get close enough to touch him, the boy spun away and ran from the hospital. Linc took after him.

The boy exploded out of the hospital doors and streaked across the park and into the parking lot. Nurses turned and heads whipped around, but no one tried to slow him.

Michael did not know where he was going. He could not have explained why he was running. He just knew he had to get away. He wanted out of the hospital. He knew he felt that he was about to burst.

Tears streamed down his cheeks. He mumbled and cursed incoherently as he ran. Behind him he could hear his father calling, 'Mike! Mike! Mike!'

Ahead of him he saw the truck. Without realizing it, he had run straight to the truck. There was no place to go. He was blocked in by the damn truck. He ran to the big rig and collapsed on the front fender. Helpless and shattered by pain and utterly confused, he wept.

When Linc caught up to him, he knelt beside the boy. He pulled the sobbing boy off the fender and did what he had tried to do in the hospital. He held him to him. He wanted to shelter him from the storm. But suddenly there was no shelter, and there was no comfort. The boy's body stiffened, and he pushed away from his father. Teary-eyed and accusing, the boy yelled, 'If you hadn't come to pick me up, I'd have been home Friday night. I'd have been with her Saturday — not out riding around . . .' He swallowed and gulped a sob and said, 'Having fun while my mother was dying.'

'You can't look at it like that, Mike,' said Linc, trying to offer some solace to the suffering child. His heart ached for the boy, but he too loved Michael's mother. He felt the pain and the loss just as Michael did, but he could only think of Michael. There was nothing he could do for her, and his own heartache was not important at the moment.

125

It was the child that mattered. He didn't give a damn about himself. Mistakes were in the past. The boy had a future. The unhappiness of the parents should not be allowed to continue in Mike. 'Nobody knew,' pleaded Linc. 'It was a sudden turn for the worse. It just happened.'

Mike stared at his father. There was no forgiveness in the eyes. The unforgiving, unyielding kid from VMI had returned.

Linc knew it. Desperately he wanted to reach the boy, convince him that they were innocent of any neglect. There should be no guilt, no accusations, not now.

'You can make excuses for anything, can't you?' said the boy nastily.

The boy glared at him, and no hint of compassion for his father could be found in his eyes. Linc had lost the boy again.

The boy glowered at Linc for a moment, then wheeled and ran away. He ran across the parking lot and into the street. Linc rose to his feet. He made no effort to go after the boy. Instead, he stood and watched Michael run down the street toward a taxi. The boy was screaming for it to stop. He waved his hands and continued to run, screaming and hollering. The taxi slowed. Linc did not move. He watched the boy get in the cab and saw it pull away and disappear in the traffic.

Linc was lost in thought. *Why did I let him go?* he asked himself. Suddenly it came to him.

I know where to find him. I know where he's going . . . the same place I'm going.

Linc stepped up and swung himself into the cab. White Wolf hurried to the other side of the truck as Linc started the engine.

The casket was the best money could buy. Flowers were piled high on the coffin. But Jason Cutler had kept the funeral service very private. There was only a handful of close friends standing with him at the graveside.

Wind ripped across the cemetery and overturned several of the flower arrangements. The women battled their dresses, trying to keep their skirts from curling up with the wind.

Cutler himself kept smoothing down his hair as the wind blew it about his head.

The priest tried to be brief. Conscious of the wind and the trouble it was causing, he read a verse of scripture at the grave and asked for God's blessings to be with Christina's family. Then he shook Cutler's hand and offered his sympathy.

Some of the mourners began to move away as Cutler moved closer to the casket. But as the casket was about to be lowered into the ground, Cutler's eye caught sight of a taxi winding its way toward the burial site. He watched it turn up the drive toward them.

Cutler whispered, 'Wait,' to the young man in charge of the burial services. The pudgy man wearing frameless glasses stopped the casket by simply raising his hand. Heads turned toward the taxi, and the mourners saw what Cutler saw — a boy in a T-shirt and wearing an Indian headband jump from the car and run toward the grave.

Without thought or consideration, he ran over markers and leaped tombstones on his way to his mother's coffin.

Cutler stepped away from the coffin and hurried out to meet the boy. But Michael ignored his grandfather in the same way he had ignored the tombstones and markers. He was on his way to his mother's casket. He ran past the mourners, the priest, and the grandfather. No one tried to stop the panic-stricken boy. He rushed up to the flower-covered casket and threw himself on the coffin and cried out for his mother.

The awkward moment grew more painful for the on-lookers as the boy sobbed loudly, 'Please, Mama, please. Don't leave me.'

Cutler moved to the boy. He reached out and touched the hysterical child's shoulder and whispered, 'Come on, Michael. Come on, son.' He tightened his grip on the boy and gently pried him away from the coffin. Michael did not resist. He lifted himself off the coffin and blinked his eyes and tried to regain his composure. Cutler slipped an arm over the boy's shoulder and led him away. Together they walked arm in arm to the waiting line of limousines.

The mourners remained silent and respectful, waiting for Cutler and the boy to pass them. When they reached the limo, Cutler helped Michael into the back seat of the car and climbed in after him. The driver closed the door and hurried around to get under the steering wheel. As the long black limo pulled away, the pudgy funeral director started the casket down into the ground.

The limo rolled down the lane toward the exit. But as it approached the street, Linc's massive truck and trailer met the limo.

Linc looked down on the limousine. In the back seat by the window, he saw Michael. The boy lifted his head an and looked up. His eyes showed no expression. He could have been looking at a brick wall.

Linc slowed the truck, but the limo continued to snake its way to the street. White Wolf watched the limo leave the cemetery. Linc did not. His head was buried in his arms over the steering wheel. He did not want to look. He knew that wherever he looked, he would see someone he loved leaving him.

When Linc walked out of the shower, he noticed the motel room's double bed. He thought about White Wolf and the Comanche practice of always sleeping with their heads facing west. He remembered kidding White Wolf about it once.

In the outside world, Linc had said, people can't always arrange it so they sleep with their head to the west. Linc had gone on to give White Wolf the example of a ship where the bunks run for and aft and the ship is sailing north or south.

White Wolf had simply countered with the statement that this was more important than Linc could understand. White Wolf had carefully positioned his bed at the exact location he wanted.

Thinking of the Indian ways, Lincoln shrugged, then tugged the motel bed away from the wall and turned it so that the pillow faced west. This simple task made him remember the things that were most important to him.

I've got to get Mike back, he thought. *But not now . . . first I have to win that title in Vegas. Even if it means giving my my fleet. The money'll let me hire lawyers, the kind of lawyers I'll need to get legal custody of my son. Without money I'll never be able to convince any court that the boy belongs with me and not his grandfather. But without Mike at my side, how can I win?*

Linc sat down and started to dress.

But if I believe that, I can't. And I'll lose everything — the contest, the money, the trucking fleet, the boy — all of the dream.

But his arguement somehow didn't convince him. He stomped down his foot, sliding it into the boot. He snatched his shirt off the bed and headed for the door, pulling the shirt on as he walked.

He stopped, his hand on the doorknob. He stood looking straight ahead at the door he hadn't opened. He knew that White Wolf would have told him not to go, but Linc felt too strongly to consider his problem with calm Indian wisdom.

The Cutler ranch was protected by a high gate of reinforced steel and miles of high heavy fence. At the entrance to the ranch was a gatehouse with two armed guards.

Linc stopped his rig at the gate and climbed down to speak to the guards. A sentry carrying an M-1 met him at the gate.

'I need to talk to Mr. Cutler,' said Linc.

'Is he expectin' you?'

'He sure is,' said Linc.

Unimpressed, the guard said, 'What's the name?'

'Just tell him Hawks' here.'

The guard walked away and stepped into the stone house and picked up the phone. Linc stared through the gate. He could see the guard talking on the phone on a two-way TV hookup. On the screen was a head shot of Jason Cutler. Cutler said very little and showed very little expression. Then the screen went blank.

The second guard turned and looked at Linc as the man who had spoken to Cutler opened the door and walked back toward him.

'Mr. Cutler says he does not wish to see you.'

Linc shrugged. 'Really? Okay, then,' he turned and hurried back to the idling truck. He climbed inside the cab and slammed the door and smiled down at the guard still standing at the gate.

He backed the rig out and turned around and headed back out the way he had entered. The guard stood by the gate with the M-1 resting in his arms. As the sound of the engine died away, the taillights disappeared in the darkness. Satisfied that he was gone, the guard strolled back to the guardhouse.

'Who do you think that guy was?' asked the guard inside.

The guard carrying the M-1 shrugged. 'Some poor bastard that got a bad deal somewhere. Thought he could just barge in on Cutler with his problem.'

'He acted like he knew Cutler.'

'I doubt that.'

In the distance the two men heard the churning of a heavy engine. They turned and saw headlights coming down the road.

Suspicious, the guard with the M-1 stepped back outside. As the sound got closer, he yelled, 'It's him again.' He walked back out to the gate, but as he took his position, he realized the rig was rolling too fast. Not only could it not stop, it did not intend to stop. He raised his weapon to fire, but the headlights were on him. There was no time. He dove to the side for cover.

The Silver Hawk smashed through the heavy gate without slowing down.

Inside the guardhouse, lights and cameras came alive. Sirens screamed as the guard hit the emergency switch.

The guard with the M-1 was on his feet firing at the truck, but the rig sped away so quickly the gunfire had no effect on the intruding tractor-trailer. Floodlights came to life like a thousand suns, turning the country night into a surrealistic netherworld of non-time.

Linc barreled the big monster resolutely down the drive to the main house. He was determined to reach his destination. The look on his face was not the zombie trance, but the glassy-eyed, crazed look of a kamikaze pilot heading for glory.

Inside the house Jason Cutler watched his arrival on a huge TV screen. On another screen the gatehouse guard sounded his warning.

'Comin' straight in, sir. There's no way to stop him now. He's inside. Repeat. He's inside.'

Calm as a summer fisherman, Cutler said matter-of-factly, 'Call the state police.'

Then he hit the remote button, killing the picture.

*

Michael was in his mother's bedroom on the second floor. He had changed his clothes. He wore a white shirt and dark blue Calvin Klein cashmere sweater with a pair of chinos and topsiders. He had retreated to his mother's room to try and grab on to some memory of her. It was as though he hoped to find in the room some personal item that would reveal to him the answers to all his questions.

He knew nothing could replace the loss, but he wanted to be where she had been. He wandered the room aimlessly, not knowing what he was looking for or what he expected to find. He only knew it was the place he wanted to be.

Suddenly the bedroom door flew open and his grandfather charged into the room.

'I want you to see for yourself just how insane he really is.'

He took hold of the boy's hand and guided him to the window.

Standing at the window with his grandfather, Michael saw the Silver Hawk speeding toward the house.

Michael's sad dark eyes did not change, but Cutler's eyes suddenly flashed alarm. He grabbed Michael by the hand and yelled, 'Goddamn idiot is gonna crash right into the house. He's crazier than those bastards in Iran. C'mon.' Leading the boy by the hand, Cutler retreated from the window.

With the sound of Eddie Rabbitt's 'Driving My Life Away' blaring full blast from the speakers, Linc buckled his seat belt.

The wheels bounced over the entrance steps and carried the big rig up to the front door. The truck smashed through the entrance of the house and into the foyer, crushing anything in its path. The walls of the house crumbled. Plaster and wood fell like rain on the invading truck. As the ceiling above the foyer gave way, dust and dirt and falling debris spilled onto the entrance floor.

The Silver Hawk rumbled on through the entry and brought the grand staircase down in slow, dangling stages. Above him the imported cut-crystal chandelier swung crazily as the plaster and support about it began to loosen and give way. At last the great hanging antique fell, smashing into bits and pieces.

Only the accumulating mass of clutter and debris finally halted the runaway rig as it chewed its way into the dining room.

But like the aftershocks of a massive earthquake, the crumbling damage of the assault continued to be felt long after the truck had finally stopped moving. Beams continued to give way and fall. Plaster and lumber continued to crack and collapse on the stalled truck below.

Smoke rose from under the hood of the truck. Water dripped from the radiator onto the carpet. Chrome dropped from the truck in strips. The air conditioner had been torn off, the truck's stacks were bent, the bumper was mangled, and the trailer was ripped with deep furrows.

Inside the cab Linc sat lifelessly staring through the shattered windshield. His eyes were only half open. He seemed unconscious. Blood oozed from a deep gash along his scalp and dripped down his face.

He shook his head, trying to clear his vision. He leaned back and sucked in his gut and unbuckled the safety belt. He felt a stabbing pain in his side. He pushed himself out of the cab and fell to the floor amid the damage.

He sat on the floor, looking about the room. He raised his head and looked up. On the second landing stood Cutler and the boy, both looking down on him.

He staggered to his feet. Weaving like a groggy fighter amid the debris, he muttered, 'Michael.' He staggered backward and fell against the truck. As he looked up at the boy, blood ran freely from the cut into his eye, dripping down his cheeks. Like a wounded animal in pain, he pleaded helplessly, 'Michael, I can't make it without you, kid. Please . . . come with me.'

Michael looked down at the bloody-faced man looking up at him. He bit his lip and tried not to cry.

Linc continued to look up. The room was beginning to spin. He staggered from foot to foot, trying to stay upright.

'I'm beggin', Michael. You're all that matters.' Then his balance gave way and his legs buckled under him and he went down, crashing among the glass and plaster.

'Portrait of a loser,' said Cutler, tightening his grip on Michael's hand.

Michael stared down at his father struggling to get to his feet.

'We can make it, kid,' mumbled Linc. But he couldn't make it to his feet. He slipped and fell once more. The grandfather said, 'Very touching. But as always, totally irresponsible.' He raised his voice and called down to Linc, 'Did it ever occur to you, Hawks, that you might have killed this boy by smashing that truck into my home?' Then he answered the question himself, 'Of course not. You never think about the consequences of your actions.'

He turned the boy to walk away, but Linc pushed himself up to his knees and roared, 'You son of a bitch. You keep out of this. Michael is my son — not yours! You had your child — a beauty too. Christina was her name.' He swallowed and threw back his head, baring his chest and soul to the heavens, and screamed, 'Look what you did to her!'

Still confused, frightened, and already in tears, Michael turned back and looked down at the sad figure below him.

'Locked her up,' yelled Linc. 'Smothered her. Well, by God, you're not going to do that to my boy. I'm taking him.'

Cool and calm as only the rich and powerful who live beyond the law can be, Cutler dropped an arm on each of Michael's shoulders.

'He's already made his choice, Hawks. At the cemetery. I didn't take him. He came to me — willingly.'

Linc struggled to get his feet under him. 'Yeah, why?' he said as he pushed himself off the floor. 'Because you made it look like it was my fault that he wasn't here when his mother died.'

'Are you denying you had him on the road all this critical weekend?'

'You knew where we were every mile of the way. When Christina had to be taken to the hospital Saturday night, you could have called me on my CB. You could have let us know. If you'd really wanted Mike to know, and be with his mother, you could have sent a chopper. But you wanted him to miss, so you could make him hate me.'

Michael looked up at his grandfather for an explanation. Cutler smiled down at Linc and shook his head.

'Put away the guns, gentlemen. They won't be necessary. Will they Hawks?'

Linc wheeled to see two state troopers approaching him with their revolvers already drawn and aimed at him.

Neither trooper dropped his gun. Instead, they moved even more carefully in on Linc.

'All right, just turn around. Put your hands behind you. Extend them. Wrists together.'

As the trooper barked the orders, Linc followed the instructions. He lifted his bloody head and glared at Cutler.

The cuffs clicked behind his back. With a shove from the trooper, he staggered across the room, but his head was still up. His eyes were still fixed on Cutler.

Michael watched as the troopers pushed his father out the hole in the wall. Turning away, he broke from Cutler and ran down the hall to his mother's room. The door slammed. The boy turned the latch and locked the door behind him. In the hall Cutler heard the sound of the lock clicking. He approached the door and raised his fist to knock, but he reconsidered, turned, and walked away.

'I'll make this brief.' Salenger, Butler's personal secretary said to Linc as they exited out onto the jailhouse steps.

'I'm listening,' said Linc, hurrying down the steps.

'As you can see you've a serious problem on your hands and, more than ever now, you'll need money for attorneys and additional expenses.'

Linc rolled his eyes, indicating that he did not need to be reminded of his growing list of legal problems.

'What Cutler wants is for you to leave the state. Don't come back, and we won't prosecute. If you decide to contest the whole matter of legal custody, you won't have a prayer — we retain the finest law firms. So that's it.'

Linc looked away.

'What do you say?'

'What does Mike say?'

'Ask him yourself — in a letter.'

They continued down the street and rounded a corner. Linc stopped abruptly, staring in disbelief. There was his truck, scratched but patched up.

Salenger, pleased with Linc's reaction, said, 'That's right. We fixed up your rig after the stupid stunt you pulled. Not because Cutler's forgiven you for any of it; he just wants you far away from Michael, and the faster the better.

'I know you'll do the right thing — the only smart thing you can do.' He reached and opened the truck door, expecting Linc to answer.

Lincoln Hawks stepped into the cab, pulled the door closed, and drove away.

*

136

Linc knew he'd have to drive nonstop to make it to Vegas in time. He didn't want to think about how this might affect his performance once he got there.

With determination, he pulled furiously at the dashboard equipment designed to strengthen his arm.

Salenger had actually believed he would give up so easily when he was so close. With that thought Linc pulled the steel grip from his jacket and started closing and opening the grip ... closing ... opening ... closing and opening ...

Michael had searched methodically every inch of his mother's suite at the ranch. The desk drawers were still pulled out. The chest of drawers had been ransacked. He scratched his head and decided to attack the closets.

The shelves were stacked with shoes and handbags. The shoes were of no interest to him. He went to work on the bags, opening and searching each one before tossing it out of the closet into a pile in the middle of the room.

He had stripped the contents of seven and discovered nothing more interesting than old concert tickets. But on opening the eighth his heart fluttered and his hands trembled. He had found the lost treasure. With a shaking hand he pulled out a packet of old letters and an envelope stuffed with snapshots.

He backed out of the closet, holding the treasures in his hands. He dropped onto the bed and spread the sought-for evidence before him. He saw stamps on the envelopes from Singapore, Japan, Indonesia, Australia, New Zealand. . . . His eyes danced. He saw that the letters were addressed to Mrs. Christina Hawks and Michael. He sighed. He took in a gulp of air and ran his hand through his hair.

At random he picked up one of the envelopes and pulled the letter from inside it. The writing was in a strong, bold hand that ran uphill on the page.

*

The letter read:

Dear Christina and Mike:

I'm in Japan. It's a wonderful country. But crowded. Boy, you wouldn't believe it. There's a lot of America here. And I was glad to see it. It's great to get on land again, but better to see signs of home.

I wish I could be there to see Mike go at the present I bought him. A box with little boxes inside. I think they call it a Chinese puzzle. I bet he'll have them all over the room and then crawl inside the big one. Take a picture of him playing with them for me.

I miss you, Christina. And I want to see my boy so much. I love you both. And one day soon we'll be together.

Trust me. And remember, I love you.

Linc.

Michael dropped the letter on the bed. his eyes were red with tears. A lump was in his throat. He wanted to fall on the bed and bawl.

At last it was clear. His mother had managed to receive a few letters from his father, and she had hidden them away. The rest had been intercepted and destroyed by his grandfather.

The devastating emotional power of the truth ripped away at his heart. His father had been telling the truth. Everything he had told him was true. The boy shook the envelope of photos out onto the bed. He ran his hand over them and fanned them out.

Immediately, he saw a picture of Linc and Christina standing arm in arm with a young baby in Linc's arms.

He looked at the picture for a long time. It was almost as if he wanted to memorize it, file it away so deeply he could never forget it. Finally he put the picture down and shoved the rest of the snapshots back into the bag without looking at them.

He picked up the packet of letters and the envelope of

pictures and crossed his mother's room to the door. He unlocked the door and quietly slipped across into his own suite.

He passed by the computer, files, and shelves of books and opened his closet and took out a travel bag. He dumped the letters and pictures into the bag. Then he opened his drawers and started haphazardly filling the bag with clothes. He did not seem to care what he took, as long as he could do it quickly. As he stuffed a pair of shoes in on top of the clothes, he paused. He turned and looked across the room at his wall poster of the Talking Heads. He crossed the room to the poster and tore it off the wall. Hidden behind the poster was a wall safe. He leaned against the wall and began to work the combination lock.

Jason Cutler stood on the second-floor landing watching workmen remove the debris from his living room. He wore a blue silk robe over his pajamas and held a snifter of brandy in his hand.

In a moment Cutler was strolling down the hallway toward his grandson's room. Dust from the debris below drifted up, tickling his nose. He sneezed and almost spilled his drink.

'Damn,' he mumbled. He rapped on Michael's door. 'Michael.' The boy did not answer him. He took the knob in his hand and attempted to turn it. The door was locked. Irritated, Cutler banged on the door even harder.

'Open this door, Michael,' he demanded sternly. There was no answer.

'Mr. Cutler.'

Cutler turned to the voice of the assistant calling him. 'The security gate is calling you.'

Cutler wrinkled his brow at the news, nodded his head to the assistant, and followed him to another wing of the second floor.

A bank of surveillance screens with multi-images flickered on the monitors. Cutler entered the room and flipped on the two-way communicator to the gatehouse.

'Yeah. What is it?' asked Cutler.

The guard on the screen said, 'Your grandson just left the compound. I wanted to check it out with you.'

'What do you mean my grandson just left?'

'He drove out, sir.'

'My grandson doesn't drive.'

'He was driving the jeep when he went out the gate.'

'And you let him?' bellowed Cutler, getting rid of the brandy snifter and peeling off the robe in one swift motion.

'Alert the police and highway patrol. Get Jim Olson on the phone. I'll be in the study,' commanded Cutler. He turned sharply and headed hurriedly for the door.

The jeep was rolling west on Highway 80. Michael was in a hurry, but he was careful not to exceed the speed limit. He wore a leather jacket, Texas Ranger baseball cap, and aviator glasses. He wanted to look as much as possible like any other eighteen-year-old kid in a jeep. To help create the image, he had placed a pillow under his seat to give him additional height in the driver's seat. On the dashboard he had taped a map of Texas and New Mexico.

He played with the controls of his CB radio until he found the same wavelength as that used by the state police. Units were already on the lookout for a jeep with Texas plates with a runaway minor driving.

Michael listened carefully to the report, but showed no signs of panic. He had expected it. So now he figured he just had to be careful. And maybe a little lucky.

He picked up the flashlight lying on the seat beside him and beamed it on a map taped to the dash. Wide red lines outlined the interstate highways, but the secondary choices — the back roads — were outlined in yellow. He had mapped a safe course into the mountains that cut across the desert toward Gallup, New Mexico.

Jason Cutler ate poached eggs, two slices of bacon, and toast for breakfast. He ate alone on the patio beside the swimming pool. He finished the toast and leaned back in his chair and sipped coffee. He checked his watch. He was growing impatient. Sloppiness had plagued him in recent weeks. Now his own attorney was late for a morning meeting.

At the sound of the footsteps on the Spanish tile, he lifted his head to see Jim Olson walking toward him. Olson was a big man with blond, thinning hair. He moved with the ease of a man who had been a professional football player. He also walked with a slight limp.

'Sorry I'm late, Jason. I've been at police headquarters.'

'Well?'

Olson pulled a chair away from the table and sat down. He placed his briefcase on the ground beside his chair.

A Mexican boy in a white jacket poured him a cup of coffee. The servant waited beside him.

'Nothing,' said Olson.

The servant hesitated. Cutler shooed the boy away with his hand.

'So what about it?' demanded Cutler.

'Nothing, zero, zip,' said Olson, his forefinger and thumb together to form a big O.

Cutler put down his cup and fell back in his chair. Gesturing wildly with his arms, he said, 'How the hell could a twelve-year-old boy disappear in a jeep? I mean there can't be a hell of a whole lot of them burning up the highways between here and Las Vegas, now can there?'

'I wouldn't think so,' deadpanned Olson as he took a sip of coffee.

'You wouldn't think so?' said Cutler, repeating Olson.

'And nobody can find him?'

'Not yet,' answered Olson, leaning forward with the coffee cup. 'But they will — don't worry. What I want you to be thinking about, Jason, is this matter of the boy's custody.'

Cutler waved at him with his hand, as if to say he wasn't interested, or at least not concerned about it.

But Olson continued, ignoring Cutler's antics. 'I've had my best people check every applicable court decision for the last one hundred years. I'll cut to the bottom line, Jason. No judge is going to award you custody of Michael. The court will give the boy to his natural father, unless Hawk cannot show support for the boy — financially.'

'Well, how the hell can he?' boomed Cutler. 'He's lost everything. Goddamn it, Jim, Michael's my son.'

Olson looked across the table at the fuming Cutler. He was neither threatened nor bothered by Cutler's power tantrum. He had seen them many times.

'I mean,' stuttered Cutler, rising up out of his chair, 'I raised him. Not that bastard Hawks. I was there for the kid — not Hawks.' He snorted and paced beside the pool. 'Me! Michael's mine. I don't give a damn what some judge says.'

'Why don't I come back a little later,' suggested Olson.

Cutler sighed, slapped his thigh, and sat back down. 'What am I going to do, Jim? The boy's my whole life. I only see the future through his eyes. If he's taken away from me, hell, man. Who wants all this shit?' he said, gesturing to the possessions around him.

'Why don't you try to make a deal with Hawks? Maybe he'll share custody. I hear he's not as unreasonable as you make him out to be.'

'Share?' grunted Cutler. 'With that goddamn trucker?' He threw his napkin across the table in anger at the very thought of sharing anything with his son-in-law.

'By God,' he exclaimed, 'I'll buy out the son of a bitch! What's he want? Five million? Ten million? I don't give a shit how much it is.'

Olson twisted his large body in the metal chair and carefully placed his weak knee under the table.

'Supoose the boy's not for sale? What then?'

Jason smiled slyly, and with a deadly finality in his voice, he said, 'Then I'll have to shoot the son of a bitch, won't I?'

CHAPTER EIGHT

Linc arrived at the New Nugget Hotel by foot, and he didn't need a bellboy for the suitcases he carried in his hands.

A banner above the door welcomed them. It read: WORLD ARM-WRESTLING CHAMPIONSHIP — WELCOME, ALL CONTENDERS.

Inside it looked like a muscle-beach convention. Big-armed brutes, shapely girlfriends, patient wives, rowdy children, and the wrestlers' friends and loyal supporters had jammed the place. They were renewing friendships, passing on their good wishes, taking odds, making bets, sizing up the competition, and just getting the lowdown on the showdown.

When Linc entered the room, a group of truckers swarmed around him and escorted him to the register. Leading the group were Ken and Brick, Linc's Tennessee steakhouse buddies.

Seeing them brought an immediate smile to Linc's face.

'Hey!' he yelled, grasping their arms and pumping their hands.

'You're here! Damn!'

'We told you we'd be here,' said Brick.

'Yeah, but . . .' said Linc.

'There ain't no buts. We said we'd be here with you. We're here,' said Brick.

As Linc signed in and the desk clerk gave them their

keys, Ken whispered, 'Hell, man, everybody and his brother's here. Even a guy from Samoa with a neck thicker than my ass.'

Brick added with some concern in his voice, 'It ain't gonna be the picnic I thought it'd be, Linc. I saw this one dude from Germany with a bicep so big it'd take two days to walk around it.'

Pinned against the desk, Linc could do little but listen to his friends' impassioned descriptions of the formidable competition they'd seen. The information did not really seem to concern him, but he listened patiently with a bemused sense of appreciation to the two truckers' observations.

'Yeah, some real bleeping monsters checkin in,' said Ken. Then, almost as an afterthought, he asked, 'How you feelin', Linc?'

Linc grinned and said, 'Like an eight on the Richter scale.'

The lighthearted, confident answer by Linc seemed to relieve the boys. They nodded their heads and grinned like kids on a cornflakes package.

Brick said, 'Why don't you weigh in? I'll take the bags upstairs.'

Linc nodded and handed Brick his suitcase. Ken gave ground and retreated with Linc, backing through the crowd like photographers trying to stay with a subject. Brick weaved his way through the people, heading for the elevators.

Linc stepped on the scales, blue-jean jacket, boots, and all. The official chewed on his cigar and leaned in close for the reading.

'One hundred and eighty-one pounds for Lincoln Hawks.' The official straightened up and said, 'I guess that puts you in with the big boys. You're gonna be a baby

146

with those buffaloes.'

'The baby usually gets his way,' said Linc dryly as he stepped off the scales.

The official adjusted the cigar at the corner of his mouth and scribbled Linc's bracket on his entry card. 'Yeah,' he said. 'They're over there.'

Linc took the card and strolled into the grand ballroom to grab a look at his competition.

He realized at first glance that the circus was in town. The contenders were there all right, but the giant room had turned into a carnival of hucksters and party animals.

Streamers decorated the walls. The competition between beer companies for wall and booth space was as fierce as the wrestling competition.

At first glance, Budweiser seemed to be winning. Their streamer covered twenty feet of wall space. But beer wasn't the only product fighting for space and consideration. Booths selling exercise equipment, ointments, vitamins, muscle raps, and even hot tubs were there to sell, sell, sell. Booths representing the Army, Navy, Air Force, and Marines were doing a brisk business too.

The registration and information booth was populated with Las Vegas lovelies personally pinning on the ID buttons.

Beside them was a bandstand with five velvet-coated rockers testing their amplifiers.

There was an announcer's booth. Its occupant was busy testing the mike system.

There was an area for the media.

There was an area for the doctors. A doctor and nurse were seated at their table.

On stage was a dais for the real celebrities who might visit the event.

In a far corner the referees in black-and-white-striped shirts huddled at a table, going over the rules.

The atmosphere was noisy and busy. And busiest of all were the wrestlers signing autographs and going over rules and strategy for the tournament.

Linc's eyes scanned the room. He was looking for only one man. Suddenly he saw him.

Bull Hurley, the world champion, was easy to spot. There was always a crowd of reporters around him, and he was three times as big as anyone in the press. There was no way for Linc to hear what the champion was saying, but it was obvious Hurley was giving the TV interviewer plenty of material for the eleven o'clock news.

Linc felt a vise closing on his elbow. When he turned to confront the source of the pain, he saw Brick's anxious face.

'So that's him?'

'That's him,' said Linc.

Both men stared at the incredible behemoth, and although neither would have admitted it, they both were asking themselves the same question: Can anyone beat this mountain who had weighed in at four hundred fifty pounds?

The jeep sped across the low bridge stretching over the dry ravine in the New Mexico desert. But at the sound of a distant droning helicopter engine, he whipped his dust-streaked face around, searching for the chopper.

He looked toward the ridge of hills behind him. There was nothing in the sky, but he was taking no chances. He turned the wheel and bounced off the dirt road he was traveling. He drove the off-trail vehicle down the slope of the ravine and turned in under the bridge.

With the engine idling, Michael waited, twisting and turning his head, trying to see out from under the bridge.

The whirling hum of the police helicopter passed over the bridge. Michael ducked his head down and waited. He could hear the helicopter moving away from him, but he continued to wait. He wanted it far, far away when he came out. He shuffled through the bag on the seat beside him and pulled out a granola bar and munched on it. He poured himself a drink from his Thermos. With not even a distant buzz of a copter in the air, he pulled the jeep out and headed back toward the road, chewing on the granola bar.

At the Las Vegas Airport, Cutler's jet rolled to a stop. His limo was waiting for him.

When the door panel of the jet opened, Cutler eagerly stepped out. Right behind him was his Aikido master, bodyguard, and trainer, the ever-present and deliberately menacing Ruker.

Baxter McBroom was waiting beside the limo. At the age of forty-four, the hard lines on McBroom's face had begun to reveal too many days in the desert sun and too many nights in the casino bars. He was Vegas casual. He wore a red silk shirt, white slacks, blue blazer. Private eyes in Vegas didn't mean class.

Cutler wasn't interested in class. He wanted what everyone wants from a detective. He wanted information.

'Is the son of a bitch still in — or out?'

McBroom said, 'He's already won his first three matches in the preliminaries.'

Cutler's face tensed with disgust. He sighed and looked at Ruker.

'If he wins his weight division tonight, he'll go into the finals tomorrow,' added McBroom. 'Where the winners of each division meet to find out who's going to be the world champion this year.'

'How much can he win?' asked Cutler.

McBroom slid his hands into the pockets of his white slacks and said, 'Well, if he takes first place in the all-weight open tomorrow night — and can beat the present

149

champion — he'll win ten thousand.'

'What's the odds?'

Jacking up his pants as he shifted his weight, McBroom said, 'Right now about forty to one against him. Nobody's beat Bull Hurley, the world champion. Not for the last eleven years, anyway.'

Cutler liked the news. It pleased him. He looked at Ruker and put a hand on McBroom's shoulder.

'Come on,' he said, ducking his head and climbing into the back of the limo. McBroom started to climb in after him, but Ruker's arm stopped him. Ruker turned and took his seat beside Cutler. McBroom waited. Ruker motioned to him. The private eye took his place next to Ruker.

The limo driver closed the back door and hurried to the front seat and headed the car for downtown Vegas.

Las Vegas at night, with its flashing neon making a daytime after dark, was the perfect setting for the arm-wrestling championships.

The New Nugget's marquee announced in bright-colored lights that the championships occupied center stage at the hotel.

Cars, trucks, campers, and motorcycles arrived regularly in front of the hotel carrying the wrestlers' families and fans.

But the waiting was over. The preliminaries were finished, and the semifinals in each weight division were winding down.

A huge crowd had gathered in the grand ballroom for the night's matches. The wives and children of the competitors, the rowdy ragtag fans and the Vegas tourists had pushed into the room, swelling it to capacity. Each man's fans had grouped themselves together to form rooting sections. They were wildly cheering.

The stage jutted from the wall with a raised dais and an

extension for the wrestlers' tables.

Above the crowd, huge TV screens had been arranged so that everyone in the crowd could see the competitors and the action close up.

On stage Johnny Cooksey, decked out in tuxedo and a hair-sprayed pompadour, prepared to announce the next match.

He jerked the mike wire and pulled the cord after him as he paced the stage like a Vegas singer.

'This is a semifinal event matching newcomer Linc Hawks, who has won his three previous matches.'

Linc was already seated at the competitors' table, pounding his palms with a bag of rosin.

At the announcement of his name, there was gentle applause, but a tiny band of truckers whooped it up. The outburst brought a grin to Linc's face. He waved a thank-you to the rowdy truckers and continued to pound his hands with the rosin.

Suddenly the crowd started to stir. Applause broke out and rose to a roar of cheers as Linc's opponent, Johnny Grizzly, clomped toward the stage.

On stage the Black Sheep — the official house band for the competition — broke into the old sixties' hippie anthem, 'If You're Going to San Francisco (Be Sure To Wear Some Flowers In Your Hair).' Grizzly had a ring of garden flowers tucked in his thick blond curls. His predominantly male fans pitched flowers in his path as he started up the stairs to the stage. The towering Grizzly took each step as if he had just conquered Mount Everest. The boy knew how to pose. He wore boots with four-inch lifts, and each time he brought one of them down on the steps, dust rose in the spotlights, to the delight of his cheering fans.

Dressed in a lumberjack costume of jeans and plaid shirt with bright red suspenders, the giant flower child finally reached the stage and turned to his adoring fans.

151

The announcer said, 'And Hawks' opponent, representing the Petaluma Association . . .' and the crowd went crazy, cheering and tossing flowers into the air. 'The three-time division winner, Johnny Grizzly.' The auditorium rocked with cheers.

Linc continued to rub rosin onto his hand. Grizzly looked down on him and bent over the table. He growled, 'I'm gonna tear you apart, turkey. I'm gonna rip your goddamn arm right out of its socket.'

His fans loved it. Linc's droopy-lidded eyes barely registered the meeting. Grizzly pulled his suspenders down and let them fall on either side of his body and took his seat opposite Hawks.

Linc positioned himself and moved his arm into the cup. The referee leaned over the table to line up the arms.

The two hands opened and locked together. The referee hovered over them, checking the grips.

'Are you ready?' he asked.

The video camera moved in for its close-up. Linc felt the spotlight aimed on him. Above him a giant TV screen mirrored his every move.

The referee shouted, 'Go!'

At the sound of the command, Linc locked his bicep and forearm to his body and torqued with an astonishing display of sheer strength, driving Grizzly's arm down toward the touch pad.

But Grizzly had come prepared. He locked his notched boot into the leg of the table, thereby locking his entire body in place. With this buttressed support, he planned to hold Linc's arm stationary and eventually wear him down as he pressed for an advantage.

But Linc had scouted Grizzly carefully, and anticipating the move, he applied reverse pressure on Grizzly's palm. Linc's arm rose dangerously close to pulling out of the elbow cup. The referee sternly pointed to him and issued a warning.

Grizzly's supporters cheered and jumped up and down as the announcer said, 'Hawk's elbow is almost out of the cup. He has until the count of three to get it fully back in the cup or be disqualified.'

The crowd quickly joined the referee in his count, 'One . . . two . . .'

But before the disqualifying three could be uttered, Linc powered his elbow back into the cup.

Immediately, Grizzly seized the moment and pushed for a drop down. Linc countered the move. Pushing his weight down onto the ball of his right foot, Linc deflected Grizzly's momentum.

The two men strained against their opponent's strength. Each pushed himself forward until there were only inches separating their faces. Straining themselves to the limit of strength and endurance, their veins swelled and turned deep purple, pulsating below the surface of the skin, like earthworms twisting in the heat of the sun. The huge swollen veins in their arms, necks, and temples seemed ready to rupture.

Suddenly, no longer able to withstand the deadlock duel of torturous arm strain, Grizzly surprised Linc with an unorthodox move, born of frustration and fatigue. He suddenly punched his fist forward, driving Linc's own fist backward, almost smacking him in the nose. But just short of bumping Linc in the nose, Grizzly stopped his forward thrust and suddenly reversed the motion and pulled Linc's arm back toward him.

The confusing, tricky move splintered Linc's rigid concentration. For a hairbreadth of a second, the maneuver diverted Linc's icy single-minded resolve. Before he could recover and reestablish his mastery of the moment, Grizzly roared a deep, guttural groan of pain and rage and shoved Linc's arm down. Grizzly's fans surged from their seats, screaming and cheering for their champion. Linc's arm inched backward, closer and closer to the touch pad.

The crowd came to its feet cheering and whistling with shouts of 'Down . . . Down . . . Down.' Seemingly spurred by his supporters, Grizzly let his concentration slip for one fatal second. Linc's arm stopped moving down. Inexorably he pulled his arm upward, then over, as he pressed Grizzly's arm down, finally pressing it to the touch pad.

The referee slapped Linc on the back, signaling him that he had prevailed. Then he extended his arm and pointed to Linc, indicating to the crowd that he had declared Linc the winner.

The announcer quickly bounded to the stage, transmitting the news, 'Hawks . . . the winner, Lincoln Hawks.'

With the official announcement, the audience erupted again with cheers. 'This semifinal loss for Grizzly means he is out of the competition.'

Grizzly's disheartened band of supporters slumped in their chairs tossing their losing bet stubs onto the floor.

Ken said, 'Grizzly didn't even get out of his weight division.'

'That's one down,' said Brick.

'Right,' said Ken. 'Linc's gonna do it. He'll go right on through the big boys without a loss. He'll easily win his weight division.'

Hidden in the back of the room, Jason Cutler rose from his seat. He was frowning. Ruker and McBroom flanked him on either side. They rose with him. Ruker did not smile. McBroom smiled a nervous half smile.

'Don't worry, Mr. Cutler,' said McBroom, eager to placate his boss. 'This was only the preliminaries. The real contest is still to come.'

Cutler snarled. 'According to your predictions, he wasn't even supposed to make it through the first round.'

McBroom fidgeted in his seat. 'That last match must

have been just a lucky upset. Hawks's luck is about to run out.'

'You'd better be right,' Cutler grunted.

Not far from the three men, the competitors for the next match entered the arena and moved toward the stage.

At the sight of the Black Cobra, a magnificently muscled black wrestler with forearms bigger than Popeye's, the crowd started to hiss and boo.

'What's this?' asked Cutler, reacting to the unruly crowd.

'Next match,' said McBroom. 'They hate him. Here you go,' he added, motioning toward the announcer, who was lifting the microphone to his lips.

'Ladies and gentlemen — the Black Co-bra.'

The big black stepped onto the stage and stood defiantly with his legs spread wide. He placed his hands on his hips and jutted his jaw out at the crowd. He wore black tights with accompanying codpiece, a sleeveless black T-shirt, and black satin cape. He pulled the cape from his shoulders and walked to the edge of the stage.

He turned his profile to the audience and curled his bicep into a burly flex. The act was immediately met with a roar of boos. But at the front of the stage a cluster of squealing female admirers rushed the stage. He looked down on them, curling his lip with contempt, and turned his head away. Again he jutted out his jaw, as if to ignore them. But as he did, he brought the silk cape in his hand up his thigh and over the codpiece, and then, extending his arm out over the edge of the stage, he let the cape drop like a parachute to the women below, scrambling for the souvenir. Then the Cobra lifted his head to the women and flicked out his tongue.

The audience answered the display with a rowdy round of Bronx cheers and boos.

Undaunted, the Cobra turned and strutted slowly across the stage.

Amid the hoots and howling, the announcer continued with his introductions. 'The Black Cobra, who will meet Mad Dog Madigan.' At the mention of Madigan's name, the crowd again roared, this time with a mixture of boos and cheers.

The announcer continued his attempt to be heard above the racket of the wild crowd. 'The winner of this match will meet Big Bill Larson.'

Larson's supporters were in their seats and cheered wildly at the drop of his name. But the announcer did not pause this time, but continued on. 'In turn, the winner of that match will meet Linc Hawks for the final determination of a champion in this weight division.'

With that news, Cutler turned and closed his eyes and nodded at McBroom, as a signal of his estimation of Linc's chances.

'As you know,' continued the announcer, All winners from each separate weight division will meet tomorrow in the All-Class All-Weight Open Competition to determine the world champion in this double-elimination tournament.'

'What the hell?' asked Cutler, at the appearance of the snarling, biting, shirtless wild man in chains.

Cutler couldn't believe his eyes.

'Mad Dog Madigan,' explained McBroom, trying to be heard above the frenzied crowd.

Madigan wore a loose-fitting pair of blue jeans with the legs cut off at the shins. The jeans were tied at the waist with a rope. He wore no shirt. His bleached white hair and unkempt beard frazzled off in all directions. His eyes glared with such an intense paleness they seemed to be bleached too.

A pair of handlers, one on either side of him and looking themselves to be escapees from the chain gang, tried to keep the Mad Dog moving in the general direction of the competitors' table.

156

The steel chains were looped around Madigan's neck and down his chest, where they tied his hands together tightly with a lock.

As Madigan snarled and all but foamed at the mouth like a rabid dog, prowling the stage and rattling his chains, the band turned up its amplifiers and ripped loose on an ear-splitting version of Steppenwolf's 'Born To Be Wild.'

Cutler buried his head in his hands with amusement at the sight of Mad Dog's trainers slapping the wild man across the face just to get him over to the wrestling table.

He turned to McBroom and asked rhetorically, 'Hawks is supposed to beat one of these guys?'

McBroom nodded knowingly.

'No way, my friend, no way,' said Cutler.

The crowd continued to snort and howl like mad dogs as the Mad Dog was jerked, shoved, and slapped to the wrestling table.

But the Cobra was not willing to forfeit center stage to the Mad Dog. As Madigan approached the table in front of him, the Cobra shoved his face to within inches of Madigan's and flicked his tongue at him with an accompanying Cobra hiss.

The enraged Mad Dog lunged at the Cobra's tongue, trying to grab it with his hands. But Madigan's handlers contained their man with the chains, quickly pulling him away from the Cobra.

The crowd loved it, clapping for them to let him go.

As they screamed, Mad Dog's eyes turned into acid, smoke-pale moons. He howled a bone-crunching, full-moon call from the wild, and brought his shackled arms up over his head, and with another eye-watering, doleful cry, he shattered the chains restraining him as if they were sugar candy.

The crowd bayed the Mad Dog howl.

In the side area off stage, Linc ignored the noise and quietly concentrated on a series of curling exercises.

The exercises demanded his full attention, calming and strengthening him.

Behind them, on the stage above, Mad Dog and the Black Cobra had finally settled down at the table. The announcer leaned in close to the competitors and described the action. The Black Sheep band laid down the background music, scoring every nuance of the bout with the proper sound.

When he finished his routine, his mind returned to the problems he'd been trying to banish.

That last match with Grizzly had been close, too close. *I'll need better concentration than that to win the championship. And all I can think of is Mike, locked in that house.*

Linc continued his exercise, doing curl after curl. An image of his mentor, White Wolf, came to him then. He knew that White Wolf would have told him to empty his mind and focus on the task at hand. Linc knew if he couldn't do this, his life would be empty from tonight on.

Behind him, the crowd was on its feet stomping and shouting at the Mad Dog and Black Cobra. Both men were strutting and posing, lapping up the adulation of their adoring fans. They used the crowd's cheers to psyche themselves to new heights of frenzy.

Linc ignored it all. He had blocked their foolishness from his mind. He had other things to worry about. He'd staked his whole future on the outcome of this contest.

The salesman had only given him seven thousand dollars for his truck, far below its true value. 'You're only going to gamble it all.' he had said. 'So what do you care?'

Linc had taken the money and bet it all on himself.

*

On stage, Mad Dog Madigan grunted piglike snorts as he pushed against the Cobra's hand. But suddenly the Cobra's hand slipped from Madigan's grip. Madigan rose from his seat howling and grunting threats at the Cobra.

The Cobra sprang to his feet, pointing a finger at Madigan and hissing epithets back at his opponent.

As the two men slapped at each other, the referee leaped between them and grabbed each man's arm. Holding the two arms in place, he strapped them together with a belt.

'You're gonna stay in harness this time,' he said. 'I've had enough.'

During the break in the action, Cutler, McBroom, and Ruker rose from their seats and headed for the aisle.

Mad Dog and Cobra jockeyed for the power position, snarling and hissing and whispering threats at each other.

In the aisle Cutler and Ruker headed for the rear exit, McBroom squeezed his way past the spectators already on their feet and standing in the aisles.

Ignoring Mad Dog and Cobra above him, he cut down an open aisle of seats that had been abandoned by the cheering fans, and headed for White Wolf and Linc.

He approached Linc with his business card extended in his hand. Linc took the card and read it quickly.

'Private dick, huh? Cutler must have sent you.'

The cocky McBroom nodded his head and said, 'Yep.'

'Whatta you want? And make it quick.'

'He wants a word with you,' said McBroom, leaning his weight on an outstretched hand against the wall. 'He's here.'

Linc glanced up, surprised by the news.

'He flew in — just for the meet,' continued McBroom. 'He's waiting for you. Presidential suite.'

Linc thought about the schedule. He knew he wasn't due to wrestle again for a couple of hours — after the women's semifinals.

If Cutler tried to detain him, Linc knew he could handle the older man.

'Okay,' said Linc eagerly. 'Let's go.'

McBroom turned and walked away without a backward glance, confident that Linc was following.

Ruker opened the door to the Presidential suite. He nodded for Linc to enter. Then, with a shift of his eyes, he sent McBroom on his way down the hall. Linc entered the room.

Linc stood inside the room, waiting for Cutler to appear. Ruker closed the door behind them. He stepped around Linc and stared at him with deep, penetrating eyes. Linc realized the mysterious giant was sizing him up and stared back.

'Come on in, Hawks,' said Cutler, calling out from the next room.

Linc shot Ruker one last departing glance and advanced into the adjoining room.

At the far end of the giant suite, which encompassed almost a whole floor of adjoining rooms, stood Jason Cutler. He had changed into a royal-blue warm-up suit and was sipping Scotch.

'Drink?' he asked.

'No,' said Linc, pausing where he was, across the suite from Cutler.

'Oh, that's right,' said Cutler mincingly, 'you're in this arm-wrestling thing downstairs.' As he moved toward Linc, he asked, 'How're you doin'?'

'What do you want, Cutler?' said Linc flatly.

'We don't have to be enemies. That ever occur to you?' said Cutler.

'I never wanted to be your enemy. I only wanted to be your son-in-law.'

With a shrug, Cutler tipped his glass and said, 'Well, nobody ever said I wasn't a son of a bitch.' He smiled his shit-kicker grin of confidence and bragged, 'I did a number on you, didn't I?'

Linc planted his feet securely under him, rocked back on his heels, and crossed his arms over his chest. Let him talk, he thought. I got nothing to say to him.

'I had my reasons,' explained Cutler. 'Right or wrong, they were my reasons. But we're way past that now — we're way on down the road. Know what I mean, Hawks?'

Linc said nothing. He waited, just staring at the man.

Cutler paused and considered for a second. He looked away from Linc, glancing at the blue sky outside the huge glass wall and said, 'With Christina gone, I have nothing left in my life now except Michael. You?' He paused again. 'You never had anything to begin with. So you have nothing really to lose — and I have everything to lose.' He turned from the wall of glass and looked squarely at Linc as he pitched him his deal 'I'll pay you one hundred thousand dollars to get on a plane or a boat tomorrow and go find someplace you can be happy — anyplace, just as long as it's out of the U.S.A.'

'And leave Mike to you?' asked Linc bitterly.

'One hundred thousand, Hawks. That's a pretty good stake for a man to start out fresh in a place like Mexico or Thailand.'

'You don't have enough money to make me give up Mike,' warned Linc.

'Give him up?' laughed Cutler. 'You don't have him, mister. He's mine. Right now, he's down on the ranch sound asleep. He's planning his future with me! Now, by God, I flew all the way up here to make you a reasonable offer.'

Linc had heard enough. He turned and headed for the door.

'Think about it!' shouted Cutler.

Linc couldn't believe his ears. He stopped and turned back to Cutler.

Cutler smiled and took a sip of Scotch. 'Now you're being smart,' he said.

'Why is it so important to you?' asked Linc, trying to understand the reason behind the sudden offer of a buyoff.

'Because I got plans for him,' snapped Cutler.

'So do I,' said Linc.

Disdainfully, Cutler asked, 'What kind of plans could you possibly have for that boy?'

'To love him,' said Linc. Then he turned and crossed the room for the door. But Ruker had circled behind him and stood blocking his exit.

Seeing Cutler's hatchet man maneuvering to stop him, Linc stopped and turned away from both men. He seemed to be considering his situation. A calmness seemed to settle over him. He stepped backward, relaxing his shoulders and arms. He cut a glance over at Ruker. Behind him he could hear Cutler moving in on him.

'All right,' said Cutler, 'I gave you my best offer, and you pissed on it. So I'll tell you what I'm gonna do. . . .'

Linc, suspecting that it couldn't be anything close to a fair shake, took a careful step to the side. He kept his eyes on Ruker, but in taking one step back to the side, he opened himself to see Cutler.

Cutler set his glass down on the table and said, 'I'm going to make sure you leave Vegas like the penniless bum you are. I'm going to break your fucking arm so there's no way you can win a penny of prize money. Then I'm going to fight you in court with every dollar I have to prove to the judge that you can't support Mike.'

'I don't fight grandfathers,' scoffed Linc, and turned and walked away.

With deadly menace in his voice, Cutler called out, 'You

162

think you're the only man who stays in top shape?'

Linc waved at his words with the back of his hand and continued walking.

'I've been studying aikido and karate for ten years, Hawks. I can beat the shit out of you with one hand tied behind my back.'

Linc shook his head, ignoring Cutler's boast. Ruker stood blocking the door. He was waiting, silent and sinister as always.

Linc paused in front of him and said, 'Am I going to have to pick you up and move you — or are you going to get out of my way?'

'Let me have him, Mr. Cutler,' said Ruker, never lifting his dark eyes off Linc.

Cutler paused and stuck out his lip and said, 'Sure. Why not? I've never really seen you in action. Let's see how a real aikido master handles an arrogant truck driver.'

Ruker moved from the door, circling in on Linc.

'Aikido master,' said Linc, circling with Ruker, moving away from him, watching his every step. 'I thought aikido was a defensive art — using the force of the opponent against the opponent. What happens, Ruker, if I just walk out the door?'

'Try it,' said Ruker.

Linc stepped toward the door. Instantly, Ruker countered the move. Gliding toward Linc with a swift, deft adjustment of his hands, he managed to grasp Linc, and using Linc's forward motion, he flipped Linc over, smashing him against the door.

Then, smoothly, with a dancer's precision, he stepped back and waited. Linc turned from the door and leaped at Ruker. But again Ruker was too quick. He slipped to the side and flipped Linc over again. This time he sent him sprawling across the suite, smashing into a table, knocking a lamp to the floor.

163

Linc felt pain in his back. His hand touched the spot in his lower spine as he came to his feet.

Meanwhile, Cutler leaned himself against the wall with his arms folded, fully enjoying the slow, methodical destruction taking place.

From the floor Linc sprang at Ruker, attempting to take him off balance. Instead, Ruker once more side-stepped the move and with minimal effort sent Linc flying back across the room, overturning a table holding a vase of fresh flowers.

Linc could feel a throbbing swelling at the corner of his right eye where his head had smacked the table. Blood trickled from the cut just above his eye. He wiped at blood dripping from his nose.

Already suffering from a loss of confidence from his defeat downstairs, Linc was uncertain of his chances. His body was shaking as he crawled to his feet and focused his blurred vision on the black-clad assassin with hands and feet as silent and swift as the wind.

Rather than try and attack the man again, Linc revised his attack plan. The calm, deadly Ruker was too much the master. Instead, Linc tried to evade the man. He knew he had a chance if he could get inside — get his hands on the man's body — but he had to distract him, break his concentration.

But instead, Ruker deliberately let Linc in close to him. Seizing his opportunity, Linc let fly with a series of elbow combinations to Ruker's neck. However, the flurry of blows only grazed Ruker's neck. He angled his body to slip out from under the blows, and moving away, he grasped Linc's left arm and twisted it up behind him. Driving the arm upward with savage force, Ruker attempted to snap the bone. A red-hot shot of pain danced up Linc's arm.

Linc squeezed his eyes shut to the pain, blocking off the

164

senses. He reached up with his free hand, and ignoring the hot balls of fire rolling up his pinioned arm, he jabbed Ruker on the pressure point of his jaw, just under the ear.

Reacting to the surge of pain in his head, Ruker dropped Linc's arm. Immediately, Linc sidestepped him and swung his left leg behind Ruker. With a quick twist he threw Ruker to the floor. Ruker bounced off the carpet with the lightness of a cat. A glint of pleasure seemed to shine from Ruker's satanic dark eyes. He readied himself for Linc's next move.

Altering his attack, Linc switched to a boxer's footwork, circling Ruker. Linc bounced on his toes, moving counterclockwise with his arms poised for a strike. He bobbed and weaved, ducking his head and faking to the right and left.

Each time Ruker tried to position himself, Linc would reverse his direction and bounce away, causing Ruker to readjust his own angle of defense.

Left . . . right . . . left . . . right . . . in . . . out . . . out . . . left . . . right, Linc continued to move, playing the butterfly. Ruker glided into place each time, cutting him off, forcing him to come to him. But suddenly, in a blinding explosion of power, Linc drove straight forward. The unexpected move caught Ruker by surprise. Linc's upper body torqued as his right knee fired into Ruker's kidneys like a jackhammer.

Ruker felt the flashbulb of pain circle his body. He pulled away, sliding backward away from Linc.

But Linc surprised the big man once more. Rather than guarding himself against a counterattack, Linc drove at Ruker, but on his approach, Linc suddenly broke into a side cartwheel. Coming off his feet to start the cartwheel, Linc's arms formed an embracing hoop for Ruker's upper body. With one arm looped around Ruker's neck and the other arm secured around his waist, Linc's speed and weight carried him over in a flip. The surprised, helpless Ruker was jerked off his feet and into the cartwheel. But as Linc came down with Ruker in his arms, he braced his knee against the floor and slammed Ruker's body across the knee. Like a dozen eggs being stepped on, Ruker's rib cage crackled and snapped. The room whirled in Ruker's head. He saw a burst of white light and then everything went black. His body sagged across Linc's knee. Linc fell backward, stunned. His upper leg was throbbing from shock. Ruker rolled down Linc's leg to the floor. Linc kicked the body off his foot. The silent giant groaned, twisting and writhing in pain.

Linc staggered backward, coming to his feet. He gasped for air and tried to steady himself. His body throbbed in pain. He was exhausted and out of breath. The room was still foggy.

As he straightened up, in the corner of his eye he caught sight of Cutler lunging at him with a lamp.

Instinctively, he ducked, but the lamp caught him on the left shoulder. The metal edge of the lamp cracked against the point of his shoulder. Pain shot through Linc's arm all the way to his fingers. He fell to his knees. He tried to lift the arm, but he felt nothing. The arm was numb and useless.

Cutler swung the lamp again at the arm, but Linc rolled away, and using his legs, he scissored his attacker's feet out from under him. Cutler toppled to the floor. Immediately, Linc was on him. Using his heel as a weapon, he drove his foot into Jason's sternum. Cutler doubled up on the floor, hugging his chest.

Linc crawled to him on his knees and rolled him onto his stomach. Pulling Cutler's leg to him, Linc levered the leg forward and across and with the leg, pulled away from the hip socket. Cutler lay on the floor like a calf ready for branding.

166

With his right hand, Linc grabbed Cutler's trachea from underneath and began choking the man to death.

Linc turned and in a fury grabbed Cutler by the front of his jacket and held him against the wall. Linc looked into his eyes and hesitated. He wanted to hit, to hurt him, to get revenge. Revenge for all the years Cutler manipulated the lives of his family, for the pain he caused even his own daughter, Christina. But most of all Linc wanted to punish him for poisoning Mike's mind against him.

Slowly Linc dropped his hands, releasing Cutler. Linc knew if he were to hurt Cutler physically, his son might never forgive him. As much as he wanted to beat up the coniving older man, he knew that the price was too high.

CHAPTER NINE

Michael saw the country gas station was closed for the night, but it was a chance. For the past two miles he'd been certain he was going to run out of gas on the highway.

At least this place had pumps. He chugged the coughing jeep into the driveway. He killed the engine at the pumps and jumped from the jeep.

Behind the station, lights were burning in a small frame house. Michael headed straight for it. He was not timid with his entrance. He hammered on the door loudly.

Troy Scott and his wife, Trudy, were watching TV. The sudden pounding on the door brought both of them out of their seats. Trudy held her chest and backed away from the door. Troy Scott picked up the loaded 12-gauge in the corner and leveled it on the door.

'Who is it?' asked Troy.

'I need gas,' shouted Michael.

'We're closed.'

'I have to get to Las Vegas right away. It's an emergency.'

Troy eased himself up to the door. He lifted the curtain and peeked out. Michael looked up at the window and pleaded, 'I need gas. Please.'

'It's a kid,' said Troy.

'Don't you go out there. I don't care who it is,' said his wife.

'I can see the driveway. He's in a jeep. I think it's just him.'

'Troy, don't do it. It's not worth the risk.'

But Troy had spotted something that was. Michael was holding a hundred-dollar bill up to the window.

'Just fill my tank. The rest is yours,' said Michael.

The man opened the door.

'Troy!' said the wife.

'I'll turn on the pump,' said Troy, pulling the door open. As he pulled open the door and started out, Michael yelled, 'Wait.'

Troy jerked the shotgun up on the boy. 'What'd you mean, wait? What's going on?' asked the man, stepping onto the porch and cutting his eyes around in every direction.

'The TV, sir. I just saw something on your TV.'

'Arm wrestling in Las Vegas, phony as hell. What about it?'

'I have to know how that match comes out. I saw my father on your TV. Please sir, I'll watch from here — just open the door.'

'Give me that hundred,' said Troy, snatching the bill from Michael. He turned the door handle and pushed the door open, revealing the TV screen.

Inside the house the woman said, 'What's wrong?'

'Nothing's wrong. He wants to see the arm wrestling. Said he saw his father.'

'Troy,' said the wife suspiciously.

'It's all right. I got the damn shotgun in my hand.'

Michael didn't hear the comments. His full concentration was on the TV screen.

Linc was at the competitors' table. His face was still bloody. His eyes were tired. There seemed to be no vitality about him.

In front of the table Mad Dog Madigan paced the stage, rattling his chains and roaring insanely.

'Shit,' said Troy. 'I'll get your gas.' The station owner

walked out to the gas pumps. Michael didn't notice.

The TV cameras moved in on the announcer. 'Now, ladies and gentlemen, for the final event of this weight class, Linc Hawks and Mad Dog Madigan.'

The crowd roared for their favorites. The camera panned across the room of screaming fanatics and came back to rest on a close-up of Madigan and Hawks locking their hands together. The referee signaled them to begin, and with a sudden growling spasm of strength Madigan drove Linc's hand toward the touch pad.

On the porch Michael said, 'Come on, come on, come on.'

The woman turned and looked at the boy mouthing encouragement to the TV screen. She considered the boy and the competitors on TV.

'Who are we for?' she asked. But Michael didn't hear her. He was riveted to the action. Linc had started pushing back. With the last bits of energy in his battered body, he slowly straightened Madigan's arm.

'C'mon, c'mon,' she urged.

In one last mighty surge of energy, Linc slammed Madigan's hand to the table.

Michael leaped into the air with a triumphant whoop.

The woman clapped her hands excitedly and smiled at Michael.

Still bouncing with joy, Michael bounded off the porch and ran across the yard to the gas pumps.

Troy was just screwing on the gas cap. 'Who won?' he asked. 'My father,' said Michael, jumping into the jeep. He started the engine and hit the gas, scattering dust and pebbles as he spun out, Vegas-bound.

Arm-wrestling zealots jam packed the New Nugget's grand ballroom for the finals. With them came the local Vegas celebrities. Flashbulbs popped and the cameras rolled.

Pulchritude and flashes of flesh vied for attention with the hunks on stage.

The Black Sheep band rocked the auditorium for a half hour before the opening match. The crowd was wired and ready for action, and the revved-up rockers had them ready to riot.

When the announcer hit the stage in an electric-blue tux, the band broke into the Elvis riff of Richard Strauss' *Thus Spake Zarathustra*, and everybody knew arm wrestling had gone big time tonight.

'Welcome, ladies and gentlemen, to the finals of the World Arm-Wrestling Championship,' barked the golden throat on his big night. The crowd roared its approval. The band belted out a fanfare. The announcer smiled and raised his hands over his head to hush the uproar.

He held up his left hand to signal that he was speaking and said, 'Of the nearly five hundred entrants, only four are left. . . .'

The band bugalooed an impromptu fanfare. The announcer laughed and continued with his introduction.

'And only one of them will walk away from here today with the title of World Champion and . . .'

He walked around the edge of the stage, holding a check above his head.

'. . . this check,' he continued, 'for ten thousand dollars.'

When he finished showing the check to the audience and allowing the TV cameras to get their close-ups, he stepped back to the center of the stage and started his introductions of the finalists.

'Now, ladies and gentlemen — and let's give these men a real Las Vegas welcome. From Georgia, the reigning king of biceps, the one and only — Bull Hurley.'

The big, burly champion lumbered onto the stage amid a tumultuous, foot-stomping, hootin'-'n'-hollerin' ovation.

Straining to be heard over the cheering crowd, the announcer said, 'And against him, the gutsiest guy who ever locked arms — from Pensacola, Florida — Carl Adams.'

Adams brought his wheelchair speeding up the ramp to the stage. The fans reacted with a boisterous welcome for the wheelchair-bound giant. He smiled warmly and waved to the crowd. Adams was a large man with huge arms and a massive chest and atrophied legs. He performed a couple of wheelies with his wheelchair and danced his pectorals for the fans. They ate it up like ice cream. In two seconds he'd stolen their hearts and made them forget their popular champion, Bull Hurley.

The announcer continued his big buildup by explaining, 'The winner will find himself against one of the next two wrestlers to be introduced. From Boston — Harry Bosco pride of the teamsters.'

Bosco climbed onto the stage. He was a tall man with long arms and large hands. He placed his hands on his hips and listened to the cheering teamsters shouting his name — 'Bosco . . . Bosco . . .Bosco . . .'

'And finally,' said the announcer, trying to be heard over the teamster chants, 'Lincoln Hawks — the Silver Hawk.'

The crowd cheered as Linc took his place beside the other men. He was dwarfed by Dean and Bosco, and in bulk alone, even Adams in his wheelchair seemed larger.

Linc smiled and raised his hand to the crowd. Ken and Brick and his trucker buddies led the cheers. As an underdog dark horse, Linc had picked up a cheering section of his own.

'Let's have a big round of applause for all four contenders,' shouted the announcer.

The audience responded with boisterous applause. The ballroom vibrated with the sounds of enthusiasm and excitement.

'We will be starting the first match in exactly five

minutes — right here, center stage, table one,' proclaimed the announcer. 'Five minutes,' he repeated, holding up five fingers to the audience.

'And let the best man win!'

The band quickly took over with a foot-stompin' farewell to the warriors. As the four men made their exits from the state, the band played the Willie Dixon blues tune 'I'm Ready.'

A few fans broke for the rest rooms and refreshment stands, but most of the crowd held their seats, clapping their hands in rhythm to the music.

When Linc walked off the stage, he headed for a quiet area behind the stage.

However, Ken and Brick and the contingent of truckers hurried for the backstage area to give Linc their best wishes.

As Linc sat down on a waiting stool in the backstage corner of the room, Ken slapped him on the shoulder. Linc sagged in pain.

Ken recoiled in horror.

'Damn lamp hit me on the collarbone,' said Linc.

'Let me see if I can work the stiffness out,' said Ken. He opened a small bag and took out a jar of Icy Hot muscle rub and started to massage the cream into Linc's shoulder.

Linc pulled away from Ken's hands, barely able to be touched at all.

'We should have the doctor X-ray that collarbone. Cutler may have broken it with that lamp.'

Linc grimaced and pulled away from his grip.

'What good will an X-ray do?'

'Tell you whether to stay in or drop out.'

'Drop out?' exclaimed Linc in astonishment. 'It's only my left arm that's hurting.'

'You can't compete with a broken collarbone,' reasoned

174

Ken. 'Any one of those three men,' he added, gesturing toward the stage, 'could drive it right into your lungs.'

'I know it's not broken, just bruised. I'll be all right.'

Brick said, 'Maybe he's right, Linc. What good's the money gonna do you if you're lying in the morgue?'

'On second thought,' Ken said, 'Linc knows his limits. We got no reason to doubt him. If he say's he's okay . . .'

Ken's eyes suddenly lit up with the excitement of a grand idea. 'If this gets out,' he said, 'know what it'd do for the odds?'

Without waiting for an answer, he volunteered his own. 'They'll drop into the basement. Think what we can make if Linc wins?'

Repulsed by Ken's crassness, Brick barked, 'You're really an asshole, Ken!'

Ignoring Brick's comment, Ken went directly to the man that mattered.

'You sure you're okay, Linc? You sure you're staying in?'

Linc's eyes rolled up and looked at the men staring at him for an answer. Gritting his teeth with the determination that had brought him so near his goals he growled, 'I'm goin' over the top!'

'That's my man,' said Ken, slapping his hands together, emphasizing his satisfaction. He turned to the truckers around him and urged, 'Come on, you guys, we gotta leak the news about Linc's collarbone. Money in the bank.'

The truckers gave Linc the thumbs-up and fanned out in all directions to break the news. Brick stood shaking his head in disapproval until Linc nodded with his head for him to get going. Brick acknowledged him with a smile and clenched fist. Then he hurried out to catch up with his friends.

Linc sat expressionless, watching him go. Quietly, he tried to work some more of the soreness from his muscles. He hadn't let on to his friends the full extent of his injuries.

175

He breathed deeply and tried to ignore the pain.

The jeep skidded against the curb and bounced to a stop in the red zone. Michael jumped from the vehicle and headed for the hotel entrance.

'Hey!' yelled the dark-haired kid in the parking attendant's uniform. 'You want it parked or what?'

Michael looked back and said, 'Yeah, sure, whatever.'

The kid in the uniform shurgged and stretched his face, as if to say. 'Listen to the big man.'

Michael didn't see the attendant's mocking imitation of him. He was on his way to the entrance of the New Nugget.

The bellman asked, 'Sir?'

But Michael didn't even pause. He pushed the door open and found himself in a strange land.

Thousands of bright white lights burned in the room. People moved in every direction. They were all busy gambling. The noise in the room was like the roar of a waterfall. Michael looked about the room. His eyes jumped from place to place like a ricocheting pinball. Then his eyes landed on the giant TV screens beaming the arm wrestling to the lobby.

On the screen Bull Hurley and Carl Adams were settling down at the table for the first of the three final matches.

The announcer's voice grew very serious. He dropped his volume to just above a whisper and said, 'Ladies and gentlemen, the winner of this match will advance to the World Championship match against the winner of the Bosco-Hawks match.'

At the announcer's words, Michael streaked through the lobby towards the cashier's window. He bumped into a middle-aged woman, whose skin was burned to the color of shoe leather. She was carrying a paper cup of quaters and smoking a Tiparillo. Upon impact with Michael the Tiparillo flew from her fingers and quarters spilled from the cup like hot chocolate slushing from a cup.

'Excuse me,' yelled Michael, not bothering to slow down.

'What the — little creep,' shouted the woman, crawling after the scattered quarters.

Michael arrived at the cashier's booth, slamming the wall hard on impact.

'Hey, watch it, kid,' said the cashier, a woman wearing haystack hair and too much green eye-shadow.

Michael quickly opened the overnight bag he carried through the lobby under his arm like a football. He pulled the stacks of currency he'd taken from the Cutler wall safe and piled it in the cashier's window.

'Ten thousand dollars on Lincoln Hawks,' said the boy.

The cashier paused in her counting and stared through the bars of the cage at Michael.

'Against the law for kids to gamble. Now, get out of here before you get in trouble,' said the cashier.

Michael's black eyes glared at the woman in the booth.

'Nothing I can do about it, kid,' she said.

'But I can,' said Ken, wrapping an arm around the boy and leaning his face in front of the cashier's window.

'He's making a bet on his old man, Stella. It's okay. You want me to hand you the money? Will that make it legal?'

But before she could answer, Brick stepped in front of the cashier bars, blocking Ken's access to the woman.

'Don't throw your money away, kid. Look!' He pointed to the TV screen above their heads. Michael turned and looked up at the screen.

On the screen was the slow-motion replay of Bull Hurley's sudden smashing victory over Carl Adams.

'On his best day your dad couldn't take Bull Hurley said Brick. 'Plus, we think he's got a broken collarbone.'

Michael's face fell blank. He turned from Brick to Ken. A flicker of decision sparkled in his eyes.

'What are the odds?' he asked.

Smiling as if it were the greatest news since frozen food, Ken said happily, 'Ten to one.'

Michael paused, pushed out his lips to show his determination, and shoved the pile of money toward the cashier.

'Madam, this gentleman is placing my bet. Ten thousand dollars on Lincoln Hawks.'

In the grand ballroom, Lincoln Hawks and Harry Bosco appeared on stage as the band played 'On The Road Again.' The truckers went wild, hooting and whistling.

Hawks and Bosco approached the table and stood on opposite sides. Bosco towered above Hawks and stared at him, glaring his contempt at the rebel trucker.

The announcer's voice crackled with excitement.

'Ladies and gentlemen — the winner of this match will face the ruling champion of arm wrestling — Bull Hurley — to determine the new World Champion!'

The crowd responded with wild applause.

'In this match the independent trucker — the Silver Hawk — Lincoln Hawks!' The applause built as Linc raised his hand to acknowledge the cheers.

'His opponent — the teamster favorite, the King of the Road — Harry Bosco!'

Bosco turned and raised his arms over his head. The teamsters cheered wildly. Continuing to turn to the corners of the room, Bosco clenched his fists and exhorted the fans to get louder.

They responded with glee. Bosco's eyes shone with a glint of madness. He turned back to the table and flexed both arms and growled across the table at Linc. Bosco's fans followed with screams and yells and growls of their own.

The primed and pumped Bosco had worked the crowd to a fever pitch.

The band shifted gears and broke into the instrumental 'Raunchy' as Bosco took his seat and lifted his arm to wrestle.

The first grasp between Linc and Bosco was not good. They released and tried again. The referee moved in and ordered the grip broken for Bosco's failure to align his arm properly with Linc's.

Frustrated by the delay, Bosco threw up his arms and started to rise from his chair. The referee quickly cautioned him to remain seated. Bosco angrily sat back down. But with his hand raised over his head he motioned to the crowd for cheers.

Suddenly they began to chant:

'Bosco . . . Bosco . . . Bosco . . . Bosco.'

Linc lifted his hand once more. Bosco gripped the hand and began to use pressure against it. But again the referee refused to signal the beginning of the match.

Instead, the referee ordered the grip broken and again warned Bosco for his failure to line up his arm.

Suddenly Bosco bellowed across the table at the referee, 'Are you gonna let me wrestle or not! Let's do it!'

The crowd screamed their delight at Bosco's outburst. They began to boo and chant.

Bosco screamed again at the ref, 'Come on, let's go!'

Again the wrestlers lined up their arms and locked grips. Immediately, the referee came between them.

Exasperated with his failure to line up his arm and please the referee, Bosco growled, 'You gonna start again? Are you gonna do it?'

The referee unexpectedly snapped back, 'Shut up, Bosco. Just get your arm down.'

Already double-pumped and wild-eyed for action, Bosco was past words. He exploded from the chair with an ear-piercing howl and grabbed the table and shook it with both hands.

179

The referee did not hesitate. He stepped forward, placed one hand on the rocking table, and pointed the other at Bosco.

'Okay, Bosco. That's one foul. Now get your arm back into the cup right now — or I'll make it two fouls!'

'You got no right to foul me,' yelled Bosco. 'You son of a bitch!'

The crowed screamed and continued to chant.

The referee did not flinch. He didn't even blink. He said, 'That's two fouls. One more and you're disqualified.'

Enraged, Bosco seized Linc's hand and glared into his eyes.

Linc stared at Bosco with dead eyes that revealed nothing.

The referee adjusted their hands. The referee stepped back and touched their hands in the signal to begin the match.

Linc, gathering all his concentration, exploded. With a lightning move he pressed Bosco's hand against the table.

Almost immediately Bosco began to shout. 'It wasn't a good start,' he yelled at the referee. 'Hawks had the leverage!'

'You lost, Bosco,' the referee replied.

'You set it up wrong!'

'It was fair.'

That was too much. The enraged Bosco surged from the table and seized the referee by the shirt and jerked him into his hands.

The frenzied crowd cheered wildly and yelled, 'Smash him! Smash him!'

The stage and ballroom were about to turn to chaos when Bosco was grabbed from behind. Bosco felt he was in the grip of an irresistible force. Despite all his efforts he found himself being pulled away from the referee.

He was turned and brought face-to-face with the

meanacing figure of Bull Hurley.

Hurley glanced down at Bosco, dwarfing him. 'You leave, Bosco, one way or the other.'

Bosco realized he was through. He looked at Hurley and quietly backed away.

Hurley kept his eyes on Bosco until he was clear of the stage. Only after Bosco's departure did Hurley glance over at Linc.

The announcer came forward. 'Would everyone — please return to their seats. Please return to your seats. Please, folks — let's settle down.'

As the noise began to subside and order was restored, he explained, 'Ladies and gentlemen, the official winner of the last match is Lincoln Hawks.'

The announcement was met with a long-sustained chorus of boos and catcalls vying with those whistling and cheering at the announcement.

The announcer dropped the microphone to his side and stepped back and waited. After two minutes of boos mixed with cheering, the enthusiasm started to flag and he lifted the mike to speak again.

'Ladies and gentlemen, let's get back to business. Now we move directly to the final event — Bull Hurley, world champion — and the sole remaining challenger, Lincoln Hawks.'

Hurley walked onto the stage and stood beside the waiting Linc Hawks. It was as if the giant had just arrived from the beanstalk to stand beside Jack.

As the crowd cheered him, Linc neither acknowledged them nor even bothered to look at Hurley. He was deep in concentration. His eyes seemed almost closed.

As the crowd cheered him, Linc neither acknowledged them nor even bothered to look at Dean. He was deep in concentration. His eyes seemed almost closed.

*

181

Linc positioned himself on his side of the giant Plexi-glass table. His face remained frozen in a mask of concentration. Tiny pulsating muscles at the corners of his jaw revealed the man's inner emotions.

Bull Hurley settled his massive bulk into the chair across from Linc. He seemed calm and relaxed. The ease with which he positioned his arm for contact clearly signaled the confidence and poise of a champion.

The referee had no trouble seating the two arms. Unlike Bosco, Hurley appeared to feel it was the easiest thing in the world.

The face of the two men were only inches apart. Linc focused in on Hurley's eyes. With the stone-cold concentration of a mentalist, Linc held Hurley locked in his stare. It was the old glare game — see who breaks. Which side of the table would hold the power side of the pyramid?

At the very moment when Linc was sure he had him ready to break, the Silver Hawk eased into a big smile.

'Thanks for jumping in last week in Tennessee. Hadn't been for that, I might not be here tonight.'

The sudden shift and friendly tribute unnerve the unsuspecting Hurley. The rigid concentration and relaxed confidence of the champion faltered. His eyes had betrayed him. Before he could recover and regain his control, the referee released their hands.

Stepping back quickly, the referee shouted, 'Go!'

Primed and ready, Linc made his move on the split second. Like a sprinter rolling with the sound of the starter's pistol, Linc's arm sprang forward, taking the advantage.

The glare game psychout smiling shift had done a number on Hurley's head. That shaking of Hurley's dominance had given Linc the precious thousandth of a second needed to springboard him into an advantage.

In that eye-blink of time needed by Hurley to recover and react to the referee's shout of 'Go,' Linc's locked bicep

182

and rigid body were already pushing Hurley's arm toward the pad.

But Bull Hurley was not only the defending arm-wrestling champion of the world, he was also a mountain. His elephantine size and strength would not allow him to go down easily. He might have lost the tip-off, but that was only the beginning, an opening skirmish in a war of power and endurance.

Hurley wedged his massive leg against the leg of the table, and like a solid wall of ice he froze Linc's blitzkrieg.

With the impact and force of two wild stags locking horns, the two men's arms stood rigid.

But slowly the massive weight and power of Bull Hurley began to take its toll.

Linc's throbbing muscles began to quiver. His rocksteady arm trembled. Linc's arm moved. Slowly, his goal-post-straight arm inched backward. At first an inch. Then, trembling and shaking, it slipped another inch. Bull Hurley's mammoth size and body strength had taken control of the match. Like a retreating army fleeing an advancing power, Linc's army was slowly surrendering its captured territory.

The crowd smelled victory. They stood cheering for Hurley to finish the match. But Linc's band of supporters yelled their support, urging him to resist.

Ken and Brick began to shout, 'Go, Linc, go!' Michael heard the anthem and joined them. Soon all of Linc's followers were shouting, 'Go, Linc, go!'

Not to be outdone, Hurley's fans countered with a shout of 'Take him, Bull. Take him, Bull!'

Straining his weary, aching muscles against the titanic force of Bull Hurley, Linc looked more and more exhausted. His pain-wracked body seemed ready to fall. With the instincts of a champion, Hurley sensed Linc's vulnerability. Savagely, he drove in for a hammer down. But Hurley's senses could not weigh Linc's courage. Linc quickly took up the slack and the lunging move for the hammer down. The sudden call to action kicked new energy into Linc's stalled system. The bolt of energy edged Hurley's wrist backward — only slightly — but the champion's crushing momentum had been checked.

Once more the two arms were frozen statues of stone. Nothing moved. Neither arm quivered. There was no trembling. Veins swollen with blood stood out on their arms. Sweat popped out on their foreheads and started to accumulate on their bodies.

The faint shudder of a sob caught in Michael's throat as the wound on his father's forehead reopened. Blood burst from the would and trickled down into Linc's eye.

Michael's lower lip stiffened. His eyes blinked. He took a deep breath.

The blood ran thickly from the gash and flowed freely into Linc's eye and down his face. He batted his eyes, but the blood had matted in his eye, half blinding him. Women began to turn their faces as the blood continued to pour from Linc's wounded head. Some covered their eyes with their hands. Others chewed their nails.

The intensity of the crowd could be seen in the faces of the audience, not in the sound of the cheering. They seemed strained to the limit, almost numb with tension.

'Incredible!' screamed the announcer. 'Already this match has gone for thirty-two seconds! And it's dead even. In a sport where victory is almost instantaneous, this is unbelievable!'

Linc had called on raw courage for his last reserves. Energy had come from somewhere, and driven by his single-minded, urgent need to win, the Silver Hawk had almost reached the end of his string. The strong man was all but broken.

Pain traveled through his body, tearing at his will to continue. His shoulder was lumped and swelling. It throbbed with pain. But his face remained chiseled with hard-rock concentration. His bicep, wrist, and chest seemed tightened to the limit. The pressure being put on them seemed more than they could withstand.

The crowd too was stretched to the limit. Suddenly Michael snapped. The young boy could take no more. He broke away and ran panic-eyed through the standing, hysterical fans mobbed near the stage. He fought his way through the spectators, pushing and shoving. Without a word of warning or excuse, he clawed his way to the stage.

Stripped of everything but courage and some unexplainable willpower that continued to direct him, Linc refused to accept defeat.

Bull Hurley began to call forth a final effort for supremacy. Whipping his head back and forth, trying to find some hidden reservoir of strength, he braced his tree-trunk legs against the table and heaved with all his power.

Linc's arm trembled like a reed shaking in the wind, but it would not relent. It would not go down.

He swung his head to the side to clear his vision and shake away the perspiration. A fine mist of blood sprayed across the stage, peppering the faces of those nearby. He brought his head back into place facing Hurley. His eyes were fierce and clear.

Michael pushed near the stage. He saw the blood droplets sprayed on the floor. He saw the blood spots on the shirt of the man beside him.

The boy grabbed an abandoned chair, pulled it to the stage, and climbed onto it.

From the lip of the stage Michael cupped his hands around his mouth and screamed at the top of his lungs, 'Take him, Dad! Take him!'

Blood trickled from Linc's nostril. The blood continued to run from the now gaping wound on his head.

The boy insanely shook his head from side to side, out

of control, screaming again and again with ear-piercing shrillness, 'Take him, Dad. Take him, Dad!'

The people around the boy did not know what to do. They stood back, staring at the convulsive child shrieking for his father.

Tears welled up in the boy's eyes, streaming down his face, his body wracked with passion, seemingly ready to explode.

Several of Linc's cheering fans joined Michael in his plea. 'Take him, Dad, Take him, Dad,' boomed across the stage.

But Linc was no longer in the New Nugget ballroom. The crowd, the lights, the TV cameras, the screams, the announcer's annoying voice, the referees' hovering shadows checking on the elbow-pad placement no longer existed. Nothing mattered — nothing existed but the *arm*. Everything else was a hazy fog. Muffled, distant sounds did not penetrate. Time itself had stopped. He was in a groggy netherworld without sound or movement.

Sweat dripped on the table from both men. The blood from Linc's head fell to the table, mixing with the sweat.

Slowly, Hurley began to force the warrior's arm down. It was slipping. Linc could feel it, but he couldn't stop it. It was moving away from him.

His body was aching. He felt sick. He felt faint and he could only half see. He was going down. He could see wild horses running free. They splashed through the ocean tide, kicking up sand along the beach. He was there with them. It was warm in the sun. Michael rode behind them on a beautiful black stallion. The boy was laughing. He pulled the boy off the horse and into his arms. They hugged each other — like father and son.

The announcer held the microphone away from his face. He knew he was shouting, but he couldn't help it.

'This incredible match has broken the one-minute mark

— but it can't last much longer. Any second now . . .'

Amid the screams, the crowd continued its chant, 'Take him, Dad.' But the screaming seemed all but over. Linc's arm continued to slowly bend backward.

But the boy was with him on the beach — father and son — and they were happy.

Michael screamed again and again, and the shrill chant somehow penetrated the dream. In the distant splash of the ocean, Linc could hear the boy's scream, 'Take him, Dad! Take him, Dad!' The fog-cutting, dream-busting echo of voices crashed against Linc's brain.

Dad! Dad! Dad! pounded in his head. He could hear the roar. The chant drummed against his temples, 'Take him, Dad! Take him Dad!'

From somewhere deep in his island dream, from somewhere in that faraway place of crystalline concentration and groggy perceptions — in that faraway place of dreams and courage — he found energy. He threw back his head and opened his mouth and from somewhere deep in the soul of Silver Hawk there exploded a primal scream so terrifying and sharp it cut through the noise of the ballroom.

The devastating wail and shuddering resurgence of power in Linc's arm stunned the straining Bull Hurley At that instant Linc swung with one unbelievable sweep of his body and went over the top. Hurley's giant arm went down, slamming against the pad.

'Touch!' shouted the referee. He slapped Linc on the shoulder to indicate victory. But Linc felt nothing in the shoulder. It was dead to feeling.

Dazed and unable to control himself, Hurley stumbled out of his chair.

Linc rose from his chair screaming. His head twisted in all directions. Moving his face like a searchlight, he looked for his son's face among the hundreds around him.

But suddenly there was no need to search — the object of the search was on the stage and in his arms.

Locked in an embrace of love that had been long denied them, Linc swung the boy around and around.

Linc and Michael's faces brightened with smiling father and son.

In the center of the crowd, Lincoln Hawks smiled.